The Mission and the Mangoes

The Mission
and the
Mangoes

Hena Parveen

www.whitefalconpublishing.com

The Mission and the Mangoes
Hena Parveen

www.whitefalconpublishing.com

ISBN - 978-1-63640-674-9

DEDICATION

To my elder brother, Hazel, who kept peeping through the door to see what I was writing!

CONTENTS

ACKNOWLEDGMENTS

The cool breeze and rustling leaves of the neem tree near my bedroom window always shield me from the hot summer sun in Chennai. They also cause me to wonder: will the leaves always rustle as they do now, or will they fade away in our future? I set about writing this novel based on that premise.

Writing about the future was something new for me; I had never tried it before. Yet, none of this would have happened without the people who helped me with my book, motivated me, and opened my mind to new ideas.

First and foremost, I am happy to express my gratitude to my supportive brother. He has always been beside me for years and still is.

To my parents, who encouraged me to read and dream. My father patiently read all the chapters, gave me suggestions, and offered criticism about the characters and the plot, helping me build the story. My mother's soothing presence gave me the liberty to spend time working on the book.

My grandparents, whose stories about the good old days helped me build the characters of Raima and her grandfather.

My friends, thank you for all the happy moments we have had and always will have!

My loving teachers in school, who taught us that life is much more than textbooks and to get up and walk ahead, even if we fall. Thank you!

A special thanks to Rekha aunty, who read the draft and gave a thorough review that helped me make many changes in the book.

To White Falcon Publishing Company for helping me realise the dream of publishing my debut work. Thank you to everyone on the publishing team, the design team, and more... it has been a wonderful time!

FOREWORD

I have read Hena's "The Mission and the Mangoes" all the way through. Very good imagination and nice language for narration. For her age, writing such a novel is really a great achievement.

After all, life started from water. So, choosing water as a theme point in her debut work is apt. Let's expect many more books from Hena in the coming years incorporating scientific principles and their effects on life.

I really appreciate her talent and effort. Let me congratulate Hena!

M. Chandra Dathan
Former Director, Vikram Sarabhai Space Centre, Thiruvananthapuram
Head of the launch authorization board of the *Chandrayaan*-1 space project.

FOREWORD

As I read this book, I was struck by two thoughts. I was quite overwhelmed by the imagination and the language of the writing of this talented young twelve-year-old author. Secondly, I felt I must have done something right as her English teacher in Grade 4!

It is indeed a great privilege for me to write a short foreword to Hena's first book. It has been an absolute pleasure to teach her as she is extremely hardworking, meticulous, sincere, enthusiastic, and a high achiever in all aspects of school life. Being her English teacher, it gave me immense joy to see that Hena is a voracious reader, because of which, her writing was something I always looked forward to reading. Her vocabulary, ideas, and how she organized her thoughts and put them into any piece of writing, be it an answer from the textbook or a piece of creative writing, demonstrated her command over the language. A very confident writer!

Her book, "Mission and the Mangoes", too, reflects the fact that she has drawn inspiration from her childhood about the setting of the story. The book talks about a very important aspect of global warming and the terrible effects it will have on the generations to come.

Hena has seamlessly woven this very real problem into a gripping futuristic fiction novel. The language used is very easy to understand and what I found extremely interesting was the sheer number of characters she has created, their names, and their roles. I particularly found the characters of Yohan Maneesh, Barfee, and, of course, the robot Alf very endearing but, at the same time, complex. The book took me on an exciting journey to the planet Tian. She has also managed to make references and connections and has been able to relate all that is happening in the world today in her book, which is set in 2050!

Based on what I have read in this book, I know that Hena is going to be a prolific writer and, I am sure, a very successful one. Thank you, Hena, for giving me this opportunity to write the foreword to your very first book. Wishing you the very best in all your endeavours.

Shonali Matthai (Kuriyan)

PREFACE

We drove on the narrow road across the paddy fields on the way to our home village in Kerala. The vast expanse of the greenery of the paddy fields reached up to the blue-hued mountains at the horizon. Not too far away stood the new bridge over the Kunthi Puzha—a river that originates in the Silent Valley—a famous tropical rainforest. Next to the new bridge, there were remains of an old bridge, with several tall stone pillars and huge rusted metal beams.

Standing on the bridge, I leaned over the thick steel bars to see the view below. The stream of water in the river was as thin as a snake. I looked at the dried-up mud on the riverbed, full of shrubs instead of long stretches of sand. There was nothing that felt alive and energetic.

The melancholy sight down the bridge brought back memories of glancing through the old family photo albums—pictures of children playing football on the silvery sand and bathing in the wide, crystal-clear stream.

On the neighbouring farm, I saw a farmer in his T-shirt and *mundu*. He was busy pulling out the weeds on his paddy farm.

"What has happened to the river?" I asked him politely. He looked at my face and gave a sorrowful smile.

"You see, years ago, in summer, we dug out truckloads of sand from the riverbed throughout the river. We built our houses, roads, and dams with this sand. We thought the riverbed would fill with sand again after a couple of years, but that never happened. So now, the river is dead. I am a farmer. I can feel the sorrow of Mother Earth! If we don't respect her, the rivers will die, and the paddy fields will never be green.

He then picked up the shovel and transferred the heap of weeds into a basket, humming a tune.

Chapter 1

RAIMA ON
THE BLACK BEACH

---

13 February 2050

The bright morning rays have lit up the entire spectrum of the village of Thumba in Thiruvananthapuram, Kerala. The surroundings no longer look very pleasant, to be honest, for the beauty that once flowed in the town's veins has now dried up. This is 2050 — a year that everyone had assumed would be awesome. But then again, you'd be forgiven for ever having assumed such a thing. After all, Thiruvananthapuram — 50 years ago — had been so attractive that one had believed its beauty would only burgeon from then on. Instead, its charm has faded; the stunning British architecture, serene beaches, and lush hills where children would take strolls and lay down on the soft grass looking upwards to the blue sky were now no more.

Twelve-year-old Raima was walking alongside the black, rough roads with a school bag clung to her shoulders. She was walking peacefully when suddenly a rotten egg-like smell blew past her, making her instantly look towards the other side — towards Menamkulam Beach.

"It wouldn't hurt me to spend a few minutes exploring the beach and finding out where this bad smell originates," she thought.

She walked down the brick steps that led to the beach and began to trudge through the muddy sand in her brand-new yellow shoes. All around her, she could see the dirty water, the muddy sand, and very few shops. The waves were moving in a smooth rhythmic rise and fall. The smell continued permeating the air and place, causing the shopkeepers to clasp their hands to their noses. They began to narrow their eyes and contort their face to emphasise just how bad the smell was. Raima, too, had to pinch her nose with her hand. She wanted to continue her stroll along the beach for a few more minutes, when a loud sound woke her from deep thought. It was the clanging of the bell from the Shree Padmanabhaswamy Temple. Although the temple was a few kilometres away, the ring was loud enough to alert the whole village. The temple's spire, otherwise called 'gopuram' in Malayalam, was covered with dust and grease. Once upon a time, the temple had been an attractive sight for locals to feast their eyes upon. Not so anymore. Raima watched the heavy wind blowing off the dust from the gopuram. The temple bell always rang at six in the evening, and it reminded her to return to her home. She walked a few steps back, stepping away from the beach, and saw a large building; it looked gorgeous. The evening sun was reflected in the shiny façade of the building. It also had a large digital arc around it that read: "The Thumba Space Research Station."

The Thumba Space Research Station was more popularly known as the TSRS.

It was a mere stone's throw away from the famous Menamkulam Beach.

The station was huge, built across five hundred acres of land — the most sophisticated and the largest space research station in the world. Its structure was covered by a plain white and thick glass tower that extended to about 19 feet. Raima could see several people working on the glass, making new decorations with construction workers still painting station parts with their paintbrushes. She could also vaguely see the outlines of the electric bikes and cars going around the station, transporting the people from one room to another.

"Why did they have to use such vehicles when they could just walk?" asked Raima to herself.

"Maybe I will ask Grandpa this question."

A grey launchpad stood near the parking area. Several massive space crafts with the name "India" printed in big black letters on the top could clearly be seen even from a distance.

Raima was staring down the beach now.

"Why is the water like this?"

She began to ask aloud some questions that her grandfather could probably have answered in a jiffy. Then, promptly, she heard footsteps coming towards her, the sound moving through the muddy sand. Raima didn't look behind her. — it was probably another person wanting to look at the beach.

"Raima?" she heard a man calling her name.

She looked back.

"Grandpa!" exclaimed Raima, hugging him.

"I haven't seen you for quite some time."

The older man chuckled. Raima's grandfather was the chief of the TSRS; his name was Yohan Maneesh, and he was the best astronomer and scientist in India.

"Sorry, dear. There has been a lot of work."

Raima smiled, understanding her grandfather's busy schedule.

"Grandpa, has anything exciting happened so far at your station?"

"No, not yet, Raima. My scientists and I are still in search of water."

****

Room 13 in The TSRS was used for observing the radio and the satellite.

Anjali, a dark-haired woman, and a junior scientist, sat with her team members staring at the computer systems in front of them. They were checking in on their technological robot.

"Well? Anything?" asked one of the senior scientists, Barfee Anthur, as if waiting for something remarkable to happen. Barfee was a dark-haired woman, a brilliant senior scientist. She was focused entirely on her work, completely oblivious to and disregarding gossip or rumours among her colleagues.

"It doesn't show any water yet, ma'am," replied Anjali.

"What did the chief expect, then? Pure water on the moon?" said Barfee.

Suddenly a robotic voice said: "Unidentified object. Unidentified object." It was coming from the central computer system.

"What's happening?" asked Barfee.

Anjali, Barfee's assistant, went closer to the central system.

She zoomed in on the unidentified object the computer programme was indicating.

"Ma'am, I think you need to take a look here," said Anjali.

Barfee, irritated, went to the central system.

"This can't be a water source, m- may be a —" stuttered Barfee. Within a fraction of a second, she felt embarrassment colour her face.

"Go get Ira," demanded Barfee.

Chapter 2

THE THUMBA SPACE
RESEARCH STATION

Ira was driving on the road along the beach, looking out at the colourless plants and the inky black sky. She looked to be in an irate mood. The electric car went through the digital arc. She could see the long antennas on the very top of the building as she shoved her head outside the window to check if the chief was still working. But Yohan's room was lit by a dim light — he must have left the station, even though he had always left a light on.

"I don't like my room to look dull!" he always said.

Ira reached the parking area and got out of the vehicle. The electric car drove towards the place near the launchpad, where all the scientists used to park their vehicles. The scientist opened the glass door.

She first showed her ID card to the electric robot. Then, she went inside as the glass doors opened. The corridors were long and deep. The scientist looked over to her side — the only things she could see were entries, gadgets and a few paintings. It looked colourful because of the blue wallpaper that decked the whole corridor of the station. The TSRS was a sophisticated facility with several passages leading to hi-tech office rooms, laboratories and control rooms. The conference rooms were housed within large glass walls. Wooden tables had also been built underneath the solid glass. The scientists used the radio and satellite rooms to observe the outer space and the satellites revolving around the earth. Ira walked past the food area, where some people were eating the food served by mechanical robots. She saw an elevator and decided to get inside without wasting time walking. She pressed the button for the fourth floor, reaching her destination in five seconds.

The room next to Ira's was the chief's. Ira needed to file a "greenhouse gas emissions" progress report. In the front was a black door, edged with golden stripes. A feeble voice came from within the room, urging Ira to step inside.

It was a big room — as big as a suite. With a wall-to-floor glass window built perfectly behind his desk, Yohan Maneesh could swivel around his chair at any time and stare at the view. There were also paintings in his room depicting the deep science of space. Yohan's was the only place in the TSRS where one could find real old paperbacks on a bookshelf. He had a bookshelf right next to his desk. The chief enjoyed the digitalised world, but he preferred the old-fashioned books.

"Ira…" said the chief. "You have come to hand me the report, right?"

"Yes, sir," said Ira.

Ira passed on the file she was holding in her hand this whole time, and the chief looked through it slowly, skimming through its pages.

"Thank you, Ira."

"You can leave now," said the chief, smiling.

Ira was about to turn her back towards the door, but something stopped her — someone knocked on the door.

"Come in," said the chief.

Behind the door stood a young lady dressed in a lab coat, T-shirt and jeans. It was Anjali, Barfee's assistant.

"Ma'am!" said Anjali. "I have been looking all over for you. Barfee ma'am is asking for you."

"What could it be now?" mumbled Ira under her breath.

Anjali smiled at the chief in an attempt to apologise for the brusque way in which she had entered the chief's office.

Anjali and Ira took the same path — through the elevator and to the first floor where Room 13 was. They both walked through the same black door.

Ira was a senior scientist. Her sister, Kiara Marzi, had gone missing in the last mission to find water. Since the supposed death of her dear sister, she had become sorrowful but had never given up on the suffering world.

"I hope it's not a frivolous matter again, Barfee. Last time you told me you saw a hippogriff on the moon," said Ira.

Barfee ignored Ira's comment as was customary with her and said, "What is this? It certainly doesn't look like the moon."

Ira gaped at the object for a minute or two, looking carefully at every little detail. Then, finally, her curious eyes focused on the oddity in front of her; she exclaimed, "It's a planet."

"A planet?" replied Barfee angrily.

"Please take a look at this, will you? It's round. Also, it's not Jupiter or Saturn!" replied Ira, trying to defend her statement.

Barfee let out a heavy sigh and asked, "Are you trying to say that we have located a new planet?"

"Yes, I am. Look, it's blue!" replied Ira

"Anjali, can you programme the robot to go closer to the object?"

Anjali obeyed and promptly brought out the controller, directing the robot forward.

"Do a scan check," said Ira.

Anjali clicked several buttons on the keyboard. It reacted by throwing several blue light beams on the planet. Then, a luscious red light showed up on the computer system screen, revealing the words: "New celestial body found".

Barfee bustled and said, "A new celestial body?"

"Anjali, aren't you supposed to follow my instructions? Try to get a look at it from farther away!" demanded Barfee.

Anjali again pressed several buttons, hoping that Barfee wouldn't make a ruckus.

The screen now showed a new image. "Water available on the new celestial body."

"Wa-water available?" stuttered Barfee.

"We need to get the chief," said Ira, hurrying off to find him.

The chief, Yohan, came and had a look at the computer. He was trembling with excitement. His hands were shaking, and his eyes widened.

"First we need to inform Shankar, then we need to contact the Indian Space Agency, and then we need to —"

He was breathless due to excitement. After five years, they had finally found another water source!

Ira thought for a while before voicing her opinion.

"Let's first inform Shankar. Then, he will know what to do," said Ira in a professional manner.

Ira walked over to a separate room to make a phone call. TSRS didn't allow the scientists to make important phone calls on their personal mobiles — only end-to-end encrypted, high-tech official communication channels were allowed.

Shankar was the head of the ISA. Ira tried to place a call to him, wondering if he would pick up as she remembered him being away on a business trip. Fortunately, Shankar was available.

"Hello, Shankar," said Ira. "We need your help."

Shankar listened to Ira's anxious yet enthusiastic explanation about this new discovery.

"AVAILABLE WATER?"

Ira could say nothing in response.

"First, the chief needs to contact the ISRT-the International Space Research Station. Then, he needs to ask them for authorisation to send a more methodical robot to investigate your lot's findings," said Shankar.

"It's nothing to worry about, right?" asked Ira

"Of course not," said Shankar, keeping his excitement down.

"My colleagues will help scour out more information about the new planet. In the meantime, gather up all the astronauts and modified spacesuits. They will be needed."

"And one more thing Ira," said Shankar.

"Yes?"

"We have observed significant new changes in the earth's reflectivity. That could potentially worsen the scenario of global warming and adversely affect our space missions. Inform Yohan of this as well."

Chapter 3

THE CHIEF SCIENTIST

Yohan was walking in exhaustion. He could have taken an electric car, but his home was close enough for him to reach by foot. The sun was setting towards the endless night, taking him back to an old memory.

Running, playing, gambolling to the hills. This had been Yohan's routine when he was young.

Yohan walked past some shops where old men impatiently stood, waiting for customers. He stopped and stared at one of the shopkeepers, an old man with a scalp of white hair, thinned almost to the point of baldness. He had an old-fashioned watch tied to his wrist — a kind of watch that locals would wear in the 2020s. The shopkeeper clasped his strong knuckles against his rough hands. The chief kept staring at him, and at last, both met each other's eyes.

The old man raised his eyebrows at the chief as if he suspected Yohan to be a high-tech burglar.

Yohan decided that he would buy a small packet of juice. So, he went towards the shopkeeper's stand, which was decorated in red; next to it was a cardboard stand with one word on it: "VERIFIED".

The officials of the world government often checked on every single shop in the various jurisdictions in a bid to ascertain if they were safe. Even though the world was made of individual countries, there was a single world government president, Marcus. He could distribute water from the imports he got from each "country leader".

"What would you like to buy?"

The shopkeeper addressed Yohan like he would any other customer when he suddenly gasped in realisation. He then broke into a smile, showing his yellow teeth and their gaps.

"Yohan, sir! I almost didn't recognise you!"

Yohan chuckled and said: "A small packet of orange juice, Niraj."

Niraj's shop was populated with various items of use — medicines, watches, tablets, food, and drinks.

He picked up a small orange pack and placed it on the glass counter.

"That will be Rs 1,000."

"Rs 1,000?" asked Yohan in surprise.

Niraj nodded.

The chief didn't want to argue and took out his expensive brown leather wallet to count out the notes.

"Thank you."

Yohan nodded and took a right turn. There were several houses in the neighbourhood, with people peering out of the windows — Yohan had no idea why. He ignored the people and continued walking. It seemed like he had been strolling around for hours, even though it had only been a few minutes. Luckily, when he looked to his right to see if he was close to his house, he could finally see it. His lazy gait gave way to an enthusiastic jog.

His house was enormous, befitting the chief of TSRS; it was white in colour and made of glass. From what the locals could see, it had six floors with several glass windows welcoming the sun's rays. The façade of the house was rectangular in shape, with several robots patrolling on the grassy lane outside the mansion.

The lane was large, about ninety acres, and had no plants. This was unusual. Several robots were cleaning the surface with the help of grey mowers.

The chief walked up to his doorstep and stood in front of an ordinary wooden door. It was decorated with a cardboard sign on the entry that said: "The Maneesh family".

Yohan threw his hand to the left, pressing a gadget on the wall and asked his granddaughter to open the door.

Suddenly, the door opened, and a girl, not very tall, with short, silky, shoulder-length hair and a smiling face appeared.

"Hi, Raima," said Yohan.

Raima smiled, letting her grandfather inside.

Yohan entered the room and walked across the lavish polished wooden floor. Raima's mother had draped the sofa in a thin golden sheet that was soft enough for a cat to sit on. Indeed, a cat hopped up and landed on all fours on the dining table. It was Raima's cat Thar, who now glided on to the golden sheet of the sofa. She rested on the couch with her claws extended.

The Maneesh family had hung up several paintings on the walls. Two of these paintings held guests' attention the most. One was a painting of Dr APJ Abdul Kalam, smiling and resplendent in his grey hair. The second one was a photograph of K Sivan, the chief of ISRO, crying on the shoulders of a former prime minister, Mr Narendra Modi. The picture had been taken immediately after the lunar module of the Chandrayan 2 mission had crash-landed.

Yohan sat on the sofa, grabbed the glass remote, turned on the TV, and leaned back.

The news headline flashed on the screen: "Dreadful Volcanic Eruption in Indonesia!"

A lady in a red suit, with straight blonde hair and thick eyebrows appeared on the screen; she looked very familiar to Yohan.

"Ah!" thought Yohan

"That's Nandini, our Shankar's assistant!"

"Nandini, could you please tell us how bad the volcanic eruption in Indonesia is?" the reporter asked.

Nandini cleared her throat.

"Yes. On the island of Java stands one of the most active volcanoes of all time — Kelut. Hundreds of people had gathered in the market nearby to attend the colourful fresh market festival, which had started at 6 pm. Suddenly, Kelut erupted and hot, red, liquid lava flowed into the neighbouring villages. Simultaneously, clouds of ash filled the whole place. Fortunately, our technological advances gave us ample warning. As a result, we could evacuate everyone to safe camps."

As Nandini explained the incident, several video clips of the volcanic eruption appeared on the screen, looking exactly as scary as Nandini had described.

"Yes," continued the reporter.

"And now, we have yet another piece of exclusive but terrible news that Nandini will explain."

Yohan stared at the video clips of lands with droughts — the corpses of different species of animals lay on the fields with no trees and no grasses.

"South Africa has been experiencing more severe droughts than usual with massive destruction of all crops. Several species of rare animals are now extinct. International President Marcus is still trying to stock up on food for the citizens. But unfortunately, there is not enough food for all the people in South Africa. Many farmers are dying as South Africa tries to battle against this obstacle."

The news ended with the screen now playing ads for expensive brands of pure drinking water. Yohan turned off the TV immediately.

Chapter 4

THE BEAUTIFUL RIVERSIDE

"Is dinner ready, dear?" asked Yohan, looking directly towards Raima.

Raima nodded.

"Grandma is in the kitchen. I will bring the plates."

Raima left the room for the kitchen while Yohan exhaustedly lay on the couch.

In a few seconds, Yohan was about to close his eyes, mindlessly drifting off to sleep....

"Dinner!" Raima yelled

Yohan woke up at once and sat up on his couch. He walked to the dining table. There was a low step to reach the dining room, where a glass table stood — modified and unbreakable.

The chief took a seat at the designer chair shaped like a diamond. It was exceptionally comfortable for anyone to sit on. Raima arrived at the dining table with a round transparent glass that was floating next to her; it was filled with eight plates.

Yohan wished he could stand up and help Raima with the plates, but he had terrible cramps in his leg.

"Better not to stand. Else, I might accidentally break the plates," Yohan thought.

The glass device itself placed all the food on the plates — fried chicken, three bowls of rice, four rolls of chapatis, three glasses of water and a medium-sized bowl of a vegetable stew.

Yohan urged his granddaughter to sit as he handed out spoons and forks and then, started eating.

An old lady emerged from the large kitchen and took a seat at the dining table. Aisha was an exceptionally determined lady. She was Raima's grandmother on her mother's side. She had white strands of hair on her head and was dressed in a plain red salwar kameez. She wore round spectacles on her nose. Her wrinkles made her look older, even though she was just about 69 years old.

"How's the food?" Grandma asked

Yohan and Raima licked the gravy with utmost satisfaction. It was undoubtedly delicious.

Grandma smiled at their inadvertent response. The family started eating, gobbling up all the food.

Raima was up to her elbows in fried chicken when she suddenly remembered to ask her grandfather a question.

"Grandpa?"

"Mhmm?" said Yohan.

"On my way back from school, I saw the Nali River. It was below the bridge."

Yohan nodded, gesturing to his granddaughter to continue.

"There's no sand at all. Isn't there supposed to be sand near a river?"

Yohan put his fork down on the table.

"Actually," said Yohan. "Years ago, when I was young, I also used to walk past that river. It was filled with glistening water, but of course, it isn't there now. At that time, sand was indeed found near the river, and I used to stand on the bank, watching the lorries come and scoop out loads of sand in sacks."

"Why did they take the sand?" asked Raima, frowning.

"Sand was used for the construction of the buildings! They wanted more buildings! Because of that, all the sand has vanished."

Raima raised her eyebrows. She now understood.

"And now, all that is remains is mud on riverbeds and wasted plants," said Raima

"Yeah," replied Yohan.

The family finished dinner in about 30 minutes. Their stomachs were quite full with all the rice and the fried chicken.

Everyone got up from their chairs and started washing their hands.

Yohan cleaned up and wondered what he could do now. Perhaps he could spend some time with Raima.

"Raima…" called out Yohan.

"Yes, Grandpa?"

"Are you busy? Schoolwork?"

Raima shook her head.

"I have finished everything"

"Let's watch a documentary?"

Raima took a step forward.

"What type of documentary?"

"Well, it's quite an interesting one. It's about the worlds of 2050 and 2010. You must be interested in that."

Raima smiled.

They both went to the living room and turned on the TV. Yohan clicked to a channel; the documentary was called "The Worldlife".

Raima watched as the documentary depicted a few pictures comparing 2050 with 2010. The voiceover of a man played over the visuals on TV.

"We now present the comparative pictures of the two modern years," the man announced.

The show went on for hours — till 9 pm — and showed several pictures. The old-fashioned voice spoke tiredly of the many changes. Raima laid her head on the couch and put her hands on her cheeks, in boredom. Even though she was usually enthusiastic about these kinds of shows, this did not particularly hold her interest.

Yohan kept pointing to the pictures, trying to interest Raima in them. It was certainly difficult for Raima to get invested in what she saw.

"Look! The rivers of 2010 were the utmost attraction in India! How beautiful they all look!" said Yohan to Raima.

Raima still sat with a sullen face and whenever Yohan would urge her to look, she would immediately change her expression to one of feigned interest.

Grandma was also watching with them from the dining table as she read a book. She had a habit of reading English and Malayalam books most of the time in the day. She might be growing old, but she refused to give up on her interests.

Raima and Yohan were still watching when they heard a sound. It was a creak from the outside door — it sounded like someone had stepped on their doorstep.

Chapter 5

MEMORIES

It was Raima's mom. She entered the room with her handbag clung to her arms, smiling.

"Didn't go to sleep, Raima?" asked Amena, Raima's mom.

Raima shook her head.

"It's not that late. Tomorrow is Saturday."

Amena went to a room and dropped off her bag. She then walked back to the living room where Yohan and Raima sat.

"A documentary?"

Amena was a tall and beautiful, bright looking lady, who was dressed in fashionable clothes. Her eyes were as brown as her mother's. One of her strongest traits was her sense of empathy.

Amena looked towards the TV. The live show continued to depict the comparisons. She sat down with the two of them, even as Grandma, who sat on the other couch finally got herself out of the book. They watched with a bit of interest, occasionally finding their minds wandering and talking to one another. Thar, Raima's cat was now jumping on the couch. She looked like she was sulking — everyone had ignored her to watch a TV show.

Finally, the show ended with the man wishing the audience "good night".

Grandma had the remote closest to her. She picked it up and turned off the TV.

"Why don't we show Raima some of our vacation photos?" asked Amena.

"Which one? Do you mean the one that we took in Malampuzha long ago?" said Grandma, in a quivering voice.

Amena nodded.

Yohan got up from the couch and went to one of the bedrooms. He came back with a couple of photographs in his hand.

Yohan was so engrossed in looking at the pictures excitedly that he paid no attention to where he was sitting.

Suddenly, he groaned. He had just fallen from the couch on to the floor with his three fellow family members looking down at him, worried.

Raima, however, looked like she wanted to burst out laughing.

The chief took his seat on the couch again and started pointing at the pictures one by one. The first picture was one with Yohan, Raima's dad and mom, and Grandma. They were happily smiling in the photo, with the stunning greenery behind them which seemed to be the highlight of the photo. The second one was a picture that Grandma had taken — of a bouquet of flowers.

"Grandma, where are these flowers from?" asked Raima, curiously.

"You may find this hard to believe —- your grandfather bought these for me," replied Grandma, looking towards Yohan in a pitying way.

"What's wrong?" asked Yohan. "Yes, I did buy these flowers."

"You look clueless about what I mean," replied Grandma. She was getting even angrier.

"BACK THEN, AT LEAST YOU BOTHERED TO SHOW SOME KINDNESS! NOW, ALL YOU DO IS WORK AT TSRS!"

Yohan had leapt against the couch. Grandma's voice was enough to wake the whole town.

"Please, both of you, don't argue like an old married couple," said Amena

"But, Mamma, they *are* an old married couple," said Raima.

Amena frowned and waved aside Raima's statement.

Yohan showed a few more pictures. They were just gorgeous — beautiful trees and plants. Many people were walking on the roads, as in the old times Amena and her mom stood in the road to take pictures.

"You know, I went to a village in Thumba a week ago!" exclaimed Yohan.

Raima raised her eyebrows curiously.

"The villages aren't like before. They aren't clean or organised. So much waste lies scattered around the land. I saw people just littering, both in public and private! The noise pollution was unbelievable too! There was so much noise — particularly on the roadways!"

Yohan showed them some more pictures; he had saved the best for last.

It was a picture of their old house, and it did not look like what it did now. It was not covered with glass. It was not filled with robots. It didn't look like the usual houses of 2050.

The house was an old-fashioned Kerala house. There was a large courtyard in the middle; various corridors had been built around it that led to the many rooms in the house. In those days, the family could watch the pelting rain come down their roofs and dance on the floor of their empty courtyard.

"I wish the house looked like this now," said Yohan, in awe.

Everyone agreed. Why couldn't everything go back to normal?

Chapter 6

PREPARING FOR
THE MISSION

Ira contacted Shankar once again to ask him another question. She then came back to the room.

"They are suggesting that we send a group of global astronauts."

"WHAT? THE LAST TIME WE SENT A GROUP OF ASTRONAUTS – THEY WENT MISSING!" yelled Barfee.

"I've already set up a team for such emergencies."

"There's already a team of astronauts set up?" asked Ira, astounded. "Who are they?"

"Well…. There's Idhant Nair, Arham Batra and Dr Sanghvi from India, Kim Young-Chul from South Korea, Femi Kimathi from South Africa, Amelia Johnson from America, Jacob Smith from

United Kingdom, Vera Ivanov from Russia — and of course, we will be adding a robot.

"So, you want to send a team of astronauts from different countries, am I right?" asked Ira.

"Yes," replied the chief.

"And the robot?" asked Ira. "Where are we going to install it from?"

"I have a few contacts. It will be ready," said the chief.

"I wish we still had our dear Abdul Kalam with us. He could have guided us," said Ira, looking wistfully at the white walls of the photo frame. The staff had decorated it with flowers, as a mark of respect.

"Oh. He passed away years ago. 2015, wasn't it?" asked the chief.

"Yes," replied Ira.

"Back to where I was."

The chief gave a slight sigh and said: "I am amazed that we have again found a new planet. But to send another group of astronauts to a risky mission…"

The chief stopped and thought for a while.

"Sometimes, it's better to take risks. We can't go on like this. Everyone's suffering. Children can't go to school without water; adults can't work adequately. I hate to think about what might happen if this goes on," said Ira with dissatisfaction.

The chief nodded in agreement. TSRS had failed their last mission to find water.

"I still think we should keep going. Let's see if this new planet can bring us some hope. We will train the astronauts better than ever," replied Ira confidently.

"Global warming is also increasing quickly, and we can see for ourselves how the glaciers are getting inundated, and the sea level is rising in Greenland."

The chief nodded.

"Quite true. We need to act. But people aren't so enthusiastic about all this anymore. It's not easy to convince people that this can help retrieve water once again."

The chief couldn't bear to think about this, especially about the time that he had given an impassioned speech on retrieving water. No one had listened to him and had simply ignored him, as if he had been telling them a fairy tale.

"I need to get on a call with the new team," said the chief and left the room.

The chief went to his office. His office was covered with a dark blue wallpaper with a thin-looking metal tab on his desk with several files on his desk. He walked over to the projector and took his pen. Then, he pressed a button on the remote, which led it to an app. He was now calling them. Eight cameras popped up on the projector, each representing the eight astronauts. The chief's camera was to the right, reflecting him as a small figure.

"Good morning. I suppose it must be another emergency?" asked Femi Kimathi, the African astronaut. Everyone was also thinking the same thing. How many missions did they have to embark on until they found a water source?

"Well, yes. Our brilliant scientists have discovered a new planet — Tian," said the chief with pleasure.

"Tian?" asked Amelia, impressed.

"Yes. Of course, I wanted you eight to go on a global mission once and for all to find water!

"I hate to say this. I desire to find water as much as you do. But there is the question of our families. The mission is precarious, am I right?" asked Arham.

"I agree with you, Arham. But we can't go living like this. The humans in the world right now are suffering! If we don't find a water source, who will? It's up to us now. Astronauts and scientists. Everyone is clinging to TSRS for hope — to send the most brilliant astronauts to space. Later on, when the risk has yielded rewards, we will find that we don't regret having taken it. Perhaps we will find that it was all worth it! A global mission to find water — that's what we need now."

The chief stopped speaking.

The astronauts seemed slightly convinced by the chief's speech.

"I am in," said Jacob, the astronaut from Britain.

Soon, others declared that they would also be part of this mission.

"Excellent. We will have a detailed meeting tomorrow at 9 am."

"Amelia and Femi — check with NASA about any new information on global warming right now. All the stations need to work together to get this done," said the chief.

"Yes, sir," said Amelia and Femi, together.

The chief ended the call. The director put the pen back on the table and looked through the window where the sun's rays shone and flickered. The sky was still luminous, despite it being past midday. He saw a dog, skipping around on the road — the first time he had ever seen a dog alive for years.

He convinced himself that he had gathered the best astronauts. This mission would not be a failure.

Now, he walked to the main room, where all the scientists were still talking in distress.

"We have another mission to complete. Get as much information as possible about Tian."

Ira grinned, knowing that the chief was satisfied with the mission.

"Tian?" asked Barfee. "That's the new name for the planet?"

"Yes," replied the chief.

Chapter 7

THE YOUNG SCIENTISTS IN SABRI HOTEL

The scientists, including Ira and Barfee, compiled data from the computer that the robot had given them. They finally handed over their findings to the chief. It was now lunchtime, and everyone sprinted towards the cafeteria. However, Ira and a male colleague stayed behind, gathering their essential files. That colleague was Ira's closest friend, Avish. He had brown hair, matching the shade of his eyes. Avish's parents had died two years ago due to scarcity of water. They had both been competent scientists.

Scientists sat down to deliberate over the type of rocket they could use for the mission. Anjali was also a rocket designer. She shared her ideas with her fellow senior scientists about a more protected rocket that could fly through even the thickest atmospheres.

Their meeting ended within one hour. Usually, at this time, the employees could return home.

"Hey, Ira, I am going to a nearby hotel to meet my sister after work. She is very enthusiastic about meeting you. Why don't you come with me? We could also check out the water status around there," said Avish.

"Sure," said Ira delighted. She would have a chance to relax and rest for the week's work. Ira's parents had been suffering from cancer for the past seven years. Constant exposure to the polluted air caused cancer in plenty of citizens. No matter the amount of effort and time invested by hospitals, nothing had been able to cure cancer in Ira's parents. They lived now in Ira's own home, on the verge of death.

Ira picked up her small office bag and slung it over her shoulders. She walked outside with Avish and set off for the Sabri Hotel.

Within a few minutes, they could see withered trees around; it reminded Ira of her parents — they had brought a young Ira to this very place for a camp. It had looked much better then and had been verdant and green. It only took them around four minutes to reach the hotel. Just as they were about to enter the hotel, an electric device stuck to the golden gates stopped them.

"Please state the reason for your arrival here."

"I've come to meet my sister," said Avish

"Will you kindly please show me your identity card?" asked the electronic voice.

Avish took out his phone and flashed his digital identity card.

"You may enter," said the electronic voice

The gates suddenly flew open, flashing them a vision of the beautiful hotel stretching out to an artificially made garden with artificial green grass. The hotel looked luxurious, and the gardeners who cared for the garden looked wearied. It took them long hours to take care of the garden and make it look perfect. They walked through the small grey brick road leading to a large hotel. An angler stood to their right shoving nets into a big box that contained various pieces of equipment.

He looked very sad.

Avish noticed him first.

"Ira, there's a fisherman there. Shall we go and ask him about the water problem around here?"

Ira thought this was a good idea and decided to go with Avish.

"Hi," said Avish approaching the fisherman first.

"Hello," said the fisherman looking a bit startled. He had a moustache and dark circles around his eyes. He probably wasn't sleeping very well.

"I am Avish, and this is Ira. We are scientists from the TSRS."

"Goodness, lord. Are you?" asked the fisherman.

Avish and Ira nodded.

"Do you need any help?" asked the fisherman, looking slightly gratified.

"Yes, we do. Could you tell us about the water problem you and the other citizens here face?" asked Avish fondly.

"Of co'se. I was putting back my net because it's challenging to find fish as there's obviously not enough clean water in the sea. One bot'le of water costs Rs 8000!" the fisherman looked very melancholic.

"I see. Do you know any water companies around here?" asked Ira.

"Yes. There's a small one just around the corner," replied the fisherman

"I see. Thank you so much. Hopefully, we will meet you often," said Ira.

The fisherman gave a small smile and went back to his work.

Avish and Ira walked towards the hotel and entered the main hall.

They went through the glass elevator, which took them only seconds and then, found themselves at the food area. There were robots all around in place of human waiters, and they were handing out food. But there was only one person in the food area as Ira and Avish entered the room. Avish's sister, Aaliyah, possessed a water company. She was one of the few people who owned such a big corporation. She sat there at one of the tables, appearing to be waiting for them.

"Hey Aali, over here!" yelled Avish.

Aaliyah at once turned her head towards them. Her face quickly widened into a smile.

Ira and Avish went to the table. Aaliyah stood up to greet them.

"You must be Ira! Nice to meet you!" said Aaliyah fondly.

"Hi!" replied Ira, smiling.

"I've heard from the chief that he has assigned a new mission that entails going to a new planet," said Aaliyah.

"She doesn't even say hi to her brother," said Avish sarcastically.

"I just talked to you a few minutes ago!" said Aaliyah laughing.

Ira laughed at their childish manner.

"By the way, how did you know about the mission? I suppose Avish must have told you?" asked Ira.

"Yohan told me first," replied Aaliyah.

"The chief? Are you both friends?" asked Ira, amazed.

"Yes, we are," replied Aaliyah with a smile.

"There are significantly fewer people here too, am I right?" asked Avish.

"Yes indeed. I had to come here because I had a meeting with a businessman from one of the water companies under my corporation," replied Aaliyah.

"What about the water around your area? Is it still holding up?" asked Ira.

"Yeah, of course," replied Aaliyah.

Aaliyah lived in a neighborhood populated by billionaires who could, of course, all afford water.

"So," said Aaliyah, sounding like she wanted to start a new topic.

"I have heard about the possibility of very severe heat waves in the coming months! Quite the news around here — it's been circulating everywhere since the ISRS declared it."

"Yes. The crisis is mainly because of the drastic changes in the amount of greenhouse gases," said Ira.

"Please, do talk in English. I cannot understand these scientific theories," said Aaliyah, laughing.

Ira and Avish gave a chuckle.

"Well," said Ira. "Greenhouse gases such as carbon dioxide are in the earth's atmosphere. These gases trap heat and don't let it escape from the earth's atmosphere to space. Greenhouse gases act like a blanket! We indeed need greenhouse gases to keep the earth warm. But if these gases increase too much, the atmosphere will get heated, causing global warming. We wouldn't then be able to live comfortably- it would be simply too hot. Water vapour is also a part of the greenhouse gases. As the earth heats, more water vapour is produced from the oceans and rivers. The more fossil fuels we use, the higher the level of greenhouse gases produced and the more the global warming."

Aaliyah and Avish nodded, pleading with Ira to continue.

"What do you mean by fossil fuel? But how is fossil fuel dangerous for us? As far as I know, fossil fuel doesn't harm much!" asked Aaliyah.

"As for that, our parents and grandparents used a lot of petrol and diesel to run their vehicles. They also used to burn coal in thermal power plants to produce energy. So, they used a lot of fossil fuels, which caused a lot of carbon dioxide to be released into the atmosphere. This was one of the main reasons for the situation we are facing now."

" Yes," replied Aaliyah, smiling.

"Mhm…I understand it a little better now," said Aaliyah.

Ira looked at her watch and flinched. It was already 3.20 pm. She had been asked to arrange for the various types of spacesuits the astronauts would wear to the mission, and she had been tasked with handing over that information by 2.50 pm!

Ira was very particular about being on time.

Chapter 8

THE PREVIOUS MISSION:
TO FIND WATER

---

19 September 2045

The morning sun beamed intermittently, only showing a hue of light. There were noises around of people gathering things they needed for the mission. The only fear that prevailed in their minds as they set off on their mission, was that of impending danger.

Aveen, the captain, was the first to reach the agency, followed by Kiara, the astrobiologist, Dr Abridhanta, Nihaan-Lunar Module Pilot, and the rest. The chief gave them essential instructions but did not say anything about the water source. Was Aveen the only person supposed to know about the water source? Was this information to be kept away from the rest of the members? Finally, at 7.30 am, they took their seats in the rocket.

By the time it was 7.50 am, the engineers had gotten off the rocket and closed the shuttle doors. The robotic voice sounded from the missile system just before Nihaan's procedure: "T minus 10 minutes to rocket launch."

Nihaan, Sidharth and Aveen checked the system to see if everything was secured. "Nervous, miss?" Sean asked Kiara.

"A little," replied Kiara.

"Want some sweets?" asked Sean in a mocking voice

"Hey!" yelled Naaz. Sean hurried off to Aveen, pretending that he was going to offer help, just so he could escape Naaz's yelling.

There were less than two minutes left for the rocket to launch.

"Everyone strap in!" said Aveen.

"Everything clear?"

"Yes, sir," replied Sidharth.

To the back of Aveen sat Naaz, who had trouble putting on her helmet as it had been quite some time since she had gone on a mission. But then, suddenly, Kiara pressed a button on Naaz's helmet, which locked over her head. Naaz looked over at her. Kiara winked at her.

Sidharth yelled, "On the count of 10!"

Everyone held on to their straps.

"Less than 5 seconds!"

"4,3,2,1."

Suddenly the rocket went up into the air and roared into the atmosphere. Everyone's helmets hit their seats. The force was emphatic. With immense tension, the rocket finally cracked itself out of its shell and propelled into space. Dr Abridhanta went to the back to look at the stunning earth through the shuttle doors.

"We have reached space," announced Sidharth.

Everyone was relieved.

"My head hurts. Gosh, what is with these helmets?" said Nihaan.

"Everyone okay?" asked Aveen.

"Yes!" everyone yelled back.

"I have to go check the engine system," said Aveen and walked away. He floated above the ground in mid-air, walking in slow motion to the engine zone. Within a few minutes, everyone was in a state of merriment. Kiara and Naaz talked about their experiences on their previous missions, while Nihaan and Arham spoke about their lives as trainees. It was their first day together on the rocket.

But the captain seemed to be a bit more distant.

Aveen was pressing some buttons on the engine system map; it showed that the path ahead was clear. He turned his back to the system.

He walked towards his fellow team members when something stopped him.

"Unidentified object found. Please move the rocket towards your left for your safety," said the robotic voice.

"What's happening?" asked Kiara, confused

Sidharth immediately turned on the radio navigation system and saw a big spaceship approaching them.

"Is that a spaceship?" asked Nihaan, even more confused.

"Something is coming towards us," said Aveen as he went closer to the radio system.

"Warning: unidentified object is interrupting the engine system. Please strap in."

The unknown spaceship was now going to hit the rocket. It was so near.

"Look out!" yelled Aveen.

This was the last conversation the ground station received from the previous mission. There had been absolutely no communication from the astronauts since then.

Chapter 9

MAHEEN FROM MADRAS MATRICULATION SCHOOL

Maheen was a fifth grader who lived in Chennai. He bounced off his bed as soon as he woke up. He had brown hair with freckles on his face. Maheen was a brilliant child; however, his best friend, Abishek, wasn't, and Maheen's mother would tell him all the time not to be friends with Abishek. His school usually began at 9 am and ended by 1 pm. He had suddenly realised that he was late by looking at his wall-mounted electric tab.

Maheen quickly went to the bathroom and got dressed. He sped off to the kitchen and grabbed the plate with the pie on it and started eating it at the table. He ran off to his room to grab his schoolbag and cruised out of the house. He pressed on the main gate of his house for an electric cab and entered the terminus. Soon, an electric taxi came, and Maheen boarded it. Within five minutes, he had reached his school. His cab stopped in front of a large, white building with a sign on it that read: "**Madras Matriculation School**".

"Hey, Maheen! I was starting to wonder why you were getting late," said Abishek, who was quite a naughty boy.

"I woke up late," replied Maheen sheepishly.

"First time it's happened, isn't it?"

Maheen nodded.

"I heard that the water system in our school is empty," said Abishek

"Empty?" asked Maheen, confused

"Yeah!"

"The —" Abishek wanted to continue his dramatic speech, but a loud noise of students rushing in as the watchman opened the gates interrupted him.

"Let's go. I will explain it all to you in class."

Abishek and Maheen went through the gates. The workers had covered the entire school boundary with glass. This glass cuboid facade was always filled with water, even though it looked like an odd place to store water. It was almost like an exhibition of water. But today, when the children looked hopefully around the boundary, they could see that there was no water.

"What happened?" murmured one of the students

"Someone must have stolen it," said one of the seventh graders.

The students entered their class, and Maheen and Abishek saw their teacher sitting at her table.

"Enter," said the science teacher, Mrs Srivaran.

They both took their seats, and watched as the other students filed in, still murmuring about the sudden disappearance of water. Then, finally, one of the students in the classroom could not keep her curiosity to her herself and yelled:

"WHAT HAS HAPPENED TO THE WATER?"

Everyone looked over to the student.

"Maria, are you okay?" asked Mrs Srivaran, looking concerned.

"O-Oh yeah, I was just curious," said Maria in embarrassment.

"Please take your seats, students!"

"The water has been taken away for purification!" said Mrs Srivaran.

The students then stopped murmuring.

"Okay. Turn to page 131 on your tabs."

All the students took out their tabs, which included chapters of every subject. Real hardback and paperback books were no longer a thing.

Mrs Srivaran started narrating why the school has run out of water.

"Do you know what a Greenhouse is?"

Maheen flew up his hand in the air, excited to answer.

"Tell us, Maheen."

Maheen stood up.

"In the olden days, there were countries with warm and cold weather. It was difficult to grow plants in winter in cold countries. So, they used a glass house to grow plants. These glass houses were also known as greenhouses."

"But then, why are these glass houses called greenhouses?" asked a student.

The teacher nodded and once again spoke.

"Sunlight could enter through the glass, heating up what's kept inside the glass house. This heat wouldn't be able to get out of the glass house. So, even if the temperature is freezing outside, there would be enough warmth inside the glass house. The plants grew happily inside the glass house. "

"Earlier, earth's citizens used diesel for running their cars and gas for cooking and heating their houses. This released lots of carbon dioxide into the earth's atmosphere. These gases in the atmosphere act like glass in the greenhouse, trapping heat."

"Earlier, there were plenty of forests in all countries. Then, the citizens cleared all the forests for farming. They also cut the trees for making houses and furniture. This is known as deforestation."

"So, how did deforestation produce global warming?"

Maheen's hands flew up once again. He interrupted the teacher's reply and said: "The plants make their food through photosynthesis. The leaves absorb carbon dioxide from the air, and the roots absorb water from the earth. With the help of sunlight, leaves then produce food. Trees also release oxygen into the atmosphere. So, trees help reduce the amount of carbon dioxide in the atmosphere and the greenhouse effect."

Some students frowned in confusion, not being able to understand. But Maheen understood it clearly.

"Why couldn't our parents use solar panels and wind turbines to produce electricity as we do now?"

"The point is, our older generations understood the danger, but they neglected the warnings. Now it's too late to correct it. We are suffering because of the negligence of our parents and grandparents."

Maheen didn't sit down. He was thinking about how the world is suffering due to global warming and water shortage. There was no water in the school, and a few hours ago, Maheen's mother had found out that their water, too, had run out. Where would they now buy water?

Chapter 10

TIAN: THE NEW PLANET

It was daybreak on Wednesday, around 8.20 am, and people in electric cars were going to school or work. Contrary to the picture of mundanity outside, however, the scientists at the TSRS were still in anguish. The water percentage had dropped even further than it usually did, in a matter of a few days. There was only one thought in their minds — were the residents of earth to blame for this situation? Had they not yet realised that they had not been taking care of earth? But no, they hadn't comprehended that. Not yet.

"The detailed meeting" was to be held today. The astronauts of the mission had travelled to Kerala the previous day. They had had to do so, because their task was coming up very soon. Idhant Nair, one of the astronauts, had travelled by an electric car to the

TSRS station. He got out of the vehicle, as its door closed automatically behind him, within a second. He began walking towards the entrance precisely when the chief entered the conference room 23.

The robotic voice had again arisen.

"Id, please"

Idhant grabbed his ID and showed it through the small camera, which the staff had attached to the glass wall.

"You may enter."

Idhant walked into the TSRS and saw a few scientists in one of the conference rooms. He could see glass around the station. He walked up the marble steps, which led upstairs with a poster above it that read, "Rooms 13-23". He walked past the rooms and stopped when he reached the respective chamber. He knocked on the door.

"You may come in," said a feeble voice from inside the room.

Idhant pushed the door open. He could see several chairs, a large table where the junior scientists kept water bottles within, and a large projector hung up not very far from the table. The chief had grey hair, with his tie wrapped around his neck and a slightly wrinkled forehead. He looked over to see Idhant, a young man who was clearly the early bird of the group.

"Good morning, Idhant. I see you have come early."

Idhant smiled.

"Good morning."

"Please take a seat."

Idhant sat in one of the chairs.

"The others will arrive in a few minutes. Femi and Vera are on their way," said the chief, satisfied. "Meanwhile, let me take you around my office."

The chief quickly got up from his chair, and Idhant started following him. It was only a matter of time before more scientists entered the station. Eventually, the chief and Idhant too entered the room after having taken a stroll outside, laughing. They were ostensibly enjoying their conversation.

As soon as the chief unlocked the door, he could see all the astronauts conversing in their chairs. They immediately stopped their conversation and turned to look over at the chief.

"Good morning, chief," said everyone in unison except Idhant and the chief.

"Good morning," replied the chief. "Let's start our meeting."

The chief quickly picked up his remote, which was on the table. Nobody seemed to have noticed it. The projector was switched on, and it shone a kaleidoscopic beam of light on the centre of the table. Everyone was sure that it would be a very informative and illustrative meeting.

"The mission will be in motion by the following Monday. We cannot delay it any further. The staff will distribute the spacesuits and other necessities to you on Saturday," said the chief.

"As you can see here…"

A great shaft of the replica of Tian was reflected as a big round ball.

"The water percentage is going down drastically, and we need to accrue water from this planet," he said, pointing at the shaft. "However, as you already know, it will be a risky mission. Therefore, you should conclude this mission within at least seven or eight weeks. We will also be sending an electric robot with you, Alf. He has been trained to help with any emergencies that may take place. Are there any doubts so far?"

Arham raised his hand, as he usually did.

"Are there active crises on Tian that we should be aware of?"

"Please wait, Arham. I will come to that," said the chief, who looked part displeased and part kind.

Yohan continued.

"The surface of Tian is quite rocky, but we have been researching at length to see if it is suitable for human life. As I say this, we are not sure if any other species lives there. But rest assured, inside the rocket, there are systems in which we will be contacting you. We will be checking on you through your body scans. We will monitor those constantly."

The chief stopped with a sigh and again continued. "Yes, dangers…"

Arham grinned and sat up in his seat.

"As I said — we are not sure about what organisms you might find there. But like we would for any mission, we will provide you with an extra scanner, which will identify almost any kind of organism."

Vera raised her hand, and the chief was startled.

"Yes, Vera, please go ahead."

"You said that it would take us seven to eight weeks to collect the water; how much time would it take us to reach the planet?"

"It will take you around three or four weeks to collect water. That might seem strangely quick for some of you, but the truth is, water can be found very effortlessly there. It's found almost anywhere on the ground," said the chief.

Everyone grew quiet.

"I will now declare the positions of your lot."

Everyone now became more eager.

"Kim-Young-Chul will be captain, Dr Sanghvi will be the team doctor, Jacob Smith will perform the role of pilot, Vera Ivanov the astrobiologist, Arham, technical pilot, Femi Kimathi, and Amelia Johnson will be the mission specialists from NASA and Idhant, the leading commander.

"You all have specific tasks to perform; please execute them properly for this mission to be a success. Even though one may deem it unnecessary for us to have pilots' positions with the help of our computers, pilots are much better than autopilot." He took another deep breath. The chief had hidden a fact from his dear colleagues and friends: he was asthmatic. His medical condition made him feel ashamed. Why? Perhaps, he thought it was a weakness and wanted to shield himself from scrutiny.

"The rocket we have created has complex engines and locations, which Alf will guide you through. And yes, there's something I wanted to tell you — and that's about the crash," the chief suddenly paused.

The astronauts had suddenly realised what he would say next — what had happened on the Previous Mission.

"As you all know —" he started coughing as if something had gotten stuck in his throat.

"Do you want water?" asked Kim-young-Chul, The Korean had spoken for the first time in the meeting.

"Yes,"replied the chief in a hoarse voice. The chief's voice had suddenly become very raspy, presumably because of the coughing.

Jacob passed a glass of water to the chief, and he drank it with a gulp.

"Thank you."

"Sorry for the inconvenience! Let's continue." Yohan had suddenly stopped as if hunting for some memory in the recesses of his brain.

"Where did I stop-ah! Yes. As you all know about the p-p-pre..."

Yohan could not bring himself to say it.

"THE PREVIOUS MISSION!" the chief suddenly yelled.

The astronauts looked astounded as though this was the very first-time they were hearing this.

"O-oh, sorry," said Yohan with a nervous laugh.

"Let me continue. You all know about the p-pre-previous mission. I must remind you that we are not dealing with the past but our present and future. We don't know whether what happened was a crash or a big explosion."

"All we need to do now is to find water."

Everyone now became silent as they struggled to put away thoughts of the previous mission. They had lost their own dear friends.

"Let's end the meeting here, shall we? I have to go join another meeting."

Everyone nodded, exchanged salutations, and walked out of the door.

Some of the astronauts had lingering doubts: -would they be able to endure this mission and return to walk on earth again? Unfortunately, it would be quite some time before their troubling queries would be answered.

Chapter 11

RECORDING 143

The days passed in a kaleidoscope of blurred images. Before the astronauts knew it, it was Thursday and they started to grow anxious as they realised it was only a few more days to their mission. The junior staff had already kept their spacesuits, food and other necessities equipped. Ira and Barfee were working on a rocket compartment, that would make the room safer and more technologically advanced. Barfee had finally concluded that there was a planet. Tian was on the news everywhere in the world. The chief had no longer wanted to keep this a secret, as he said to Barfee:

"This is a global mission. We need everyone to know that we have some hope!"

The chief was sitting in his office, like he would any other day. The chair he sat on was a soft brown one. He liked it; he'd had it for almost five years now. He now settled in to do some light reading. *The Newslet*, a daily newspaper, would pop up daily on citizens' tabs around the world, and the chief was an avid reader too. He held his electric device in his hand and scrolled down to the trending number one story:

A New Hope!

16 February 2050

Scientists and astronomers in the Thumba Space Research Station have risen to the Number 1 Station again. Five years ago, The MN-03 was sent by the same station to find water. However, the inconceivable happened — the astronauts on the mission went missing. On 13 February, just a few days ago, the scientists at the TSRS found another planet, TIAN, and established it as their new water source. 80 per cent of our water needs can be met by this new planet, says scientist Ira Marzi, who has also contributed to the last mission. The chief of the TSRS, Yohan Maneesh, said:

"We have a group of incredible astronauts ready to go on this mission, and we shall make sure that this mission is a success."

The team is made up of eight people, including the famous Kim-Young-Chul and Vera Ivanov, who have contributed to many space missions in the past. The other astronauts are Idhant Nair, Arham Batra, Femi Kimathi, Dr Sanghvi, Amelia Johnson, Jacob Smith, and Alf, the technological robot. According to the staff at TSRS, the necessities are in place, and the mission will take off on 20 February. Let's hope it turns out to be a success. Tun to page number 3 to read more about Tian.

— Newslet editor, Zohan

The chief suddenly got a call from Shankar, who was the official Ira had contacted after the discovery of the planet. Yohan slid away from the tab of the Newslet and proceeded to take the call.

"Good morning," said Shankar

"Good morning, and to what do I owe this pleasure?" the chief asked, apprehensive.

"Sir, one of the scientists at your station, Avish has sent us the preliminary information about the planet."

"Go on," replied the chief

"Just 10 minutes ago, Maria, my colleague, hunted for radio transmissions on the planet and — there seems to be one."

"What?" said the chief astounded.

"Yes, I will send the transmission to your system. Do check with your scientists."

"I will, thank you," said the chief and hung the phone.

He ran to the main door of his office and opened it. In a few minutes, he had walked into the speaker room, next to his office. He went up to the mic and pressed a button on it.

"Attention, everyone! I request Ira Marzi, Avish Zakir, Barfee Anthur and Anjali Shair to come to the main system, room 13. I repeat — room 13."

He again pressed the mic button, which turned it off, and he ran to room 13. He opened the door to the room and waited for the scientists to come. The scientists had run to the room as well. They opened the door and looked at a slightly worried chief.

"Sir, is everything okay?' asked Ira.

"Shankar just contacted me." He was not looking at their faces and was continuously pacing around the room, causing his dear scientists to turn this way and that, to look at him.

"It turns out they have found a radio transmission from Tian."

"A radio transmission?" asked Barfee. "Let's play it then! It must be valuable."

Barfee went to the system and pressed a few buttons, which threw up hundreds of recordings; she clicked the most recent one — "Recording 143."

She played it.

At first, they could hear nothing but what sounded like rocks being pushed away. Then, it stayed the same for almost three minutes, even as the scientists still stood in their places.

"I think that it's just the atmosphere —" said Ira.

"KEEP QUIET," said Barfee in a hoarse whisper.

The silence had gone for another two minutes, when the unexpected happened. A loud screeching voice arose from the recording. The scientists put their hands over the ears.

"Reduce the volume!' shouted the chief to Barfee.

She quickly reduced it. The loud screeching voice did turn down a bit, but it still sounded louder than anything they'd heard before. The voice on the recording seemed to be saying something: "Fuguie Marzika?" What was it? The scientists paid more attention and focused single-mindedly on the words. It became clear now: "FAzuKi MaRfuZu".

The recording suddenly stopped as it came to its end.

"Replay the recording from the screeching voice," said the chief in a confused voice.

Barfee again played the recording with the same loud screeching voice and the words: FAzuKi MaRfuZu.

"I don't understand! There isn't a single living organism on that planet!" said Barfee, as befuddled as the others.

"The computer cannot always accurately establish the existence of living organisms on unknown planets," said Yohan.

"What kind of living organism would be able to live on a planet like that? We had to have sustainable spacesuits for the astronauts to survive!" said Avish.

"Should I run this recording through our files to see if it matches any sound in outer space?" said Anjali, who had spoken for the first time since they had entered the room.

"Yes, Anjali, please do. Make sure you use computer 13 in room 5." Anjali nodded and left.

"What are we going to do now?" said Ira in a high-pitched voice.

The chief continued: "We can't tell anyone about this, not even the astronauts. It would distract them from their mission."

Chapter 12

SAFETY OF OUR ORB

---

15 February 2022

Safety of Our Orb

"*Preserve and cherish the pale blue dot, the only home we've ever known,*" *said Carl Sagan.*

There are some recent damages, as I will talk about. The following incidents took place yesterday on the 14ᵗʰ of February. We at Newslet will give you updates.

Tahiti, the largest island in French Polynesia, has been facing multiple floods and droughts each season. Citizens of this island have been recording the recent events and sending them over to the IG (International Government).

Honshu, an island in Japan, has also been suffering from floods continuously for the past week.

The World Resilience Project (WRP) has appealed yet again for various countries to contribute more water. So far, it has selected Australia, China and Japan to contribute to the organisations newly made by the COP 26. The president of WRP Azid Maya made a statement to that effect at 5.15 pm, during which he said:

"More systems and organisations have been made to avoid excessive carbon dioxide and droughts!"

Climate change has now resulted in scorching temperatures, causing deadly heatwaves along the coasts of Canada and wildfires in America — as confirmed by the scientists at the KKS space research station and the TSRS. Greenhouse gases have been rising to levels of 80 and above. Climate change is no longer in the control of humans! The greenhouse gases have altered the weather patterns and the ecosystems.

The COP, also known as the Conference Of The Parties, aims to reduce climate change. The UN Climate Change has set up more organisations over the past two weeks to initiate some change; unfortunately, nothing has improved matters.

We come to the end of this article by concluding with this piece of exclusive news:

A severe flood has occurred in China, and the dark, brown water has been pushing around several towns and cities, flooding many high-tech buildings! More than 5 million citizens of China have been affected by the flood, while the rest have been evacuated to safe camps.

"The Cal fire" also occurred at 7.25 pm today in Boston, America. Many Americans have been injured and sent to hospitals. Scientists are still researching the occurrence of this fire, and the editors who take over after this broadcast will upload the updates on the following Newslet.

The most surprising news that Newslet has for today, though, is a statement made by the TSRS that Indian people now only have one tree left for its one million humans because of the reckless cutting down of trees. This is now the lowest rank in the whole world for trees per humans! America has 28 trees per million people, Egypt- has no trees and Australia-29 trees in the whole country. In 2020, India had 28 trees for each person, America had 716 trees for one person, Egypt had one tree for one person and Australia had 3,266 for one person!

In the next five years, climate change will become far worse than it is now, with no trees to see us through those tragic years.

Recently, many Indian women have been selected for missions to space — including many global missions. The latter have chosen some of India's best female astronauts and the most experienced ones.

— Kiaan, Newslet editor

Chapter 13

THREE DAYS BEFORE
THE MISSION: MN-04

Savin, a professional robot making company in Munnar, Kerala —

Scraping. Keyboard clicking. Continuous talking. A computer chair scraped the floor and swivels around. There couldn't have been a better place to make robots. Just then, a robotic voice sounded.

"Hello, I am Alf and —"

A brown-haired man — Ishir — burst out of his computer chair. He had two faces and would simultaneously act kind and rude.

"CAN'T YOU MAKE THAT ROBOT STOP TALKING! IS THIS HOW HE IS GOING TO REACT WHEN THOSE FAMOUS ASTRONAUTS TALK TO HIM? IS THIS

HOW HE IS GOING TO HELP THEM FROM DANGER!"

Suddenly, the man fixing the wires at the back of Alf's mechanised back leapt up.

"Jeez," he said.

"What should we do?" whispered a woman to Nand, the person who was patching the wires.

Nand kept silent.

"No!" came the whispering voice of Ishir again. He was looking through a window which was near Alf.

Ishir is from Kashmir, a beautiful place that had been voted the most popular place visited by tourists in 2022. But of course, that was years ago. It had become less and less attractive as the years had gone by. The land had become progressively drier. All the gorgeous apple orchards around Kashmir were now in a bad state. Even Gulmarg — a coveted spot for skiing — was suffering; the snow caps on the mountain had melted.

"HE'S COMING!" his voice now become all squeaky.

"Who's coming?" asked one of the workers at the shop.

"The chief of TSRS!"

All the workers gazed into each other's faces. Ishir had not told them about Yohan coming. Then, suddenly, the door opened, revealing none other than the chief himself. He was wearing a tiny blue suit and boots, his thinning grey hair barely reaching his forehead. Yet his moustache grew well, and it now twitched as his face broke into a happy smile. The door creaked open once again, and the sound of a soothing voice came from outside — it sounded like someone humming a tune. Ishir bent his body over to glance at the person who was entering. It was a girl with short hair; she was hopping on the floor happily. Raima?

Ishir had suddenly recognised the young girl — it was Yohan's granddaughter.

"Ah, yes! My granddaughter was quite interested in meeting Alf! I am sure you know Raima?"

"Yes, yes!" exclaimed Ishir awkwardly and he gave a nod of greeting towards Raima. She gladly smiled at him.

"Well, I am most curious to see Alf! You do realise that the mission will be held on the 20th?" Yohan said, suddenly looking at Ishir.

"Oh yeah, of course!" replied Ishir.

"P-Please come here."

Ishir walked over to where Alf was standing, and the chief followed him. He had a fearsome smile. His squeaky voice and his angry face had dissipated.

"Well, yeah, this is him," said Ishir.

The chief took a step forward to face Alf.

He walked over to one of the robots, covered with a metal casing. Alf had glassy blue eyes, a narrow body, and a small red object wilting from his ears, causing him to talk like a human being. He looked almost like an actual human.

"This is Alf."

The chief walked over to Alf, who looked better than ever. He was smiling brightly, and the chief put him to the test by setting up a dialogue with him. Alf wonderfully passed "Robotic Function Test," also known as RFT.

"Alf is perfect for us. Send him to the station."

"Yes, Chief."

"Goodbye then, Alf!" exclaimed Raima.

By night, Alf had arrived at the station, and all the scientists were curious to see the robot who would help them in the most incredible mission.

Ever since the day the chief had received the mysterious recordings from Tian, more and more recordings from the planet were getting intercepted. Maybe it was better, for now, to ignore them, the chief concluded.

Chapter 14

ONE DAY BEFORE
THE MN-04 MISSION

Two days had passed. There was now only one day until the mission, MN-04. At the same time, all the scientists were vexed and afraid that they might do something wrong. One scientist was the most vexed among them; Ira spent most evenings pacing in her room.

"What about the spacesuits? Are they ready?"

"Ira! Don't fret so much. Everything is ready," Avish replied unhurriedly and calmly.

"That's the same thing the junior scientist told me, and someone smashed one of the bottles!" said Ira

"It's just a bottle. We have many bottles."

"This might be the only mission during which we might find water. I don't want this kind of silly mistake happening!" said Ira.

"We all know that — be calm."

"Then, there are those recordings that the chief hasn't even informed the astronauts of. What will happen if they find such things when they reach?"

"Tomorrow is the mission, Ira."

Ira gave a big sigh. Then, unexpectedly, the door of the radio room opened. Avish glanced at the person who had entered. He had assumed that it was the chief, but no — it was Kim Young-Chul, the captain of mission MN-04. He had opened the door without even knocking.

"Young-Chul," said Ira. "Is everything okay?"

Kim Young-Chul stared at both scientists.

"The recordings. The chief told me."

Ira and Avish stood frozen in the same spot. They stood that way for quite some time until Ira spoke.

"W-What?" stuttered Ira.

Young-Chul kept quiet.

Avish took a step towards Young-Chul.

"Did he?"

Young-Chul nodded.

"Well, I don't see any reason for him not to tell you. You are the captain, after all. But he didn't tell us that he would inform you," said Avish.

"Yes," said Ira decisively.

"Did you have any questions about it?"

Young-Chul looked down to the floor and looked up again.

"Ma'am, I don't see why the chief can't inform the other astronauts."

Avish took a step back.

"Young-Chul, it's just that — uh — the chief might not have a lot of faith in the other members. It's not that he doesn't trust the others, but as you are the captain, he might have felt more confidence in telling you," said Avish in one breath.

"What if the others think that I have —" Young-Chul started to say something but stopped.

"You have what?" asked Ira.

"Never mind," Young-Chul said with a small smile.

"Just forget this whole thing," said Ira. "At least you know about this; warn others if you think it's urgent."

Young-Chul nodded once again.

"You may leave if you'd like," said Ira.

Young-Chul nodded and left the room.

As soon as he left the room, Ira faced Avish.

"I can't believe the chief did such a thing."

"I know — I know," said Avish

"I guess he made the right decision."

Avish looked at the door once again and faced Ira.

"Let's go before Barfee comes; otherwise —"
Once again, the door flew open. A thin figure was reflected in the shadows, leaning against the wall.

"Was someone talking about me?" Barfee asked with a smirk on her face.

Avish gulped.

"I have been standing outside the room for quite some time."

Ira looked at her.

"Then how did you hear us talking so well? Oh, that device you use!"

Ira made a disgusted face.

"You must have also heard about Young-Chul."

"Obviously," said Barfee, still smiling.

"Okay, okay!" said Ira. "I don't want to waste time. So please, both of you, help me check on the rocket once more."

Avish and Barfee groaned.

Chapter 15

VIEW FROM ABOVE

The morning appeared greyish as the astronauts looked up at the sky. Finally, once and for all, they could start their mission. Anxiety clouded their minds as they entered the station. As expected, Idhant Nair came first, followed by the other members — Jacob arrived three minutes late. There were hundreds of people waiting outside the station and throwing their weight at the bars. They all were eager to see the rocket take off. Yohan once again called all the astronauts for a quick review meeting, during which he repeated the instructions.

It was 8.30 am when the chief decided that the astronauts could take their places inside the rocket. They entered the rocket as they had earlier to look inside. There had been some gorgeous additions — seven compartments, food and storage areas, spacesuit areas, a sleeping area and a small room with a projector used for calls; it was the best rocket made so far in history. Vera Ivanov, the Russian astronaut and astrobiologist looked to her side and leapt for a second. There stood Alf. The robot looked at her and said: "Good morning." He greeted all the astronauts and automatically told them to take their places. Jacob took the first seat near the computer system — Idhant right beside him. Kim Young-Chul was behind Idhant, followed by the other astronauts on his back and to his right. Alf took his place in the seat at the back.

"20 more minutes," said Idhant. He was going to be doing the timing commands.

Suddenly, Barfee entered the rocket.

"Everyone good?" asked Barfee.

Amelia Johnson, who was sitting right beside where Barfee was standing replied: "Yes, ma'am."

"Great," Barfee said. "Umm — so, the chief has given you all the instructions and the compartments here — just go through it again. I shall go now; good luck."

Everyone awkwardly said thanks. Minutes passed, and they all fastened their seat belts.

"One more minute to go," said Idhant.

Everyone wore their helmets and sat up straight in their seats.

Seconds and seconds passed.

"Five seconds!"

"3,2,1."

The rocket roared and soared upwards. Successfully, the rocket found itself in space in a matter of seconds — astronauts held tightly to their seats.

"We are in space," said Kim Young-Chul, looking front and back towards his members, checking to see if they were alright.

Arham Batra heaved a sigh of relief.

"Now, if you don't mind," said Arham. "Please let me through. I need to check the computer system."

"Already?" asked Femi Kimathi.

"Yes," replied Arham.

Dr Sanghvi started looking at information on her device — each of them had one in their hands — analysing the members' statistics.

"Oh god, I want to take off my helmet. I am suffocating inside it!" said Femi.

Just as Femi was about to take his helmet off, everyone yelled.

"NO!"

"O-Okay."

"Don't do that!" said Vera. "We are in orbit!"

"There's no problem in taking it off!" argued Femi.

"Please, everyone!" yelled Kim Young-Chul.

"Femi, please wear your helmet; we can't risk anyone taking it off."

"Okay, Captain. As you wish," said Femi.

They all started talking about the most random things they could think of. Young-Chul, Idhant, Jacob, Dr Sanghvi and Arham didn't speak but continued working.

Arham returned from his check and said: "Guys, you need to take a look outside!"

"What happened?" asked Amelia, worried

"Nothing to worry about; look at our earth."

All the astronauts unlocked their belts, got up from their seats and went to a long, slender glass window. Earth. How dreadful it looked. The water was not blue — instead it was all a grey-blackish mess. There were burning clouds, and the countries had long shifted from their original places to different spots on the map. Their earth which was once so beautiful, had become the worst they could imagine.

"Wow. Look at the state of it," said Idhant.

"I know, right," said Arham.

Jacob looked towards the robot beside him, staring into wonderless space. Alf looked like he was dreaming.

"Uh — Alf? Robot?"

Alf stood up at once.

"Yes, sir!"

"Come along with us. Look at our earth!" said Jacob, pointing to the window.

Alf took some steps forward, leaning on to the other astronauts' backs and staring over them.

"It is beautiful," said Alf. Alf said this despite the earth looking so discernibly terrible.

Dr Sanghvi let out a giggle, and Alf returned to his seat.

"The emotions of this robot — wow," said Young-Chul.

"In 2020, the Covid pandemic made the world shut down their transportations and factories," Young-Chul said again after a few seconds of silence.

"Within a few weeks of the pandemic, the air was clear enough for the people of Delhi to see the top of the Himalayan mountains! The people could have learnt their lesson then and created clean earth. But they never learnt from their mistakes."

Young-Chul took a deep sigh.

Two hours passed, and all the astronauts became engrossed in their respective work.

The rocket was being worked by Jacob, with Idhant assisting him. Arham was administering the computer systems. Femi and Amelia were doing miscellaneous tasks, and Dr Sanghvi was checking the spacesuits. Vera went through the map the chief had provided her with — it had additional information about Tian. Alf was studying the storage areas and adding more stuff to them. The one person who was monitoring them all was Young-Chul. The first lot of work had to be finished by noon before they could consume their lunch. They were all already tired. There were three weeks left during which the work had to be continuously ticked off the list by the members.

At noon, they ate their lunch and rested for a bit, before continuing their work again.

Chapter 16

EARTH NOW FAR AWAY!

Before they knew it, it was eight at night, and the astronauts had consumed their dinner. They took their seats and started working and checking off items on the staff's checklists. They all took turns checking the verification of space station and vehicle software and developing tools. However, Femi and Amelia were still doing extra tasks. As they were mission specialists from NASA, they had to do a few functions that NASA had given to them. The two astronauts had brought an extensive and slender device with them. As they took it out from their bags, everyone gasped at its bluish colour and its elaborate electronic switches.

Jacob raised his eyebrows in question towards Femi and Amelia.

"Checking on the disappearances on earth, obviously," replied Amelia, who was now extending the device.

"Oh, this is a NASA task!" said Dr Sanghvi, grinning.

Femi nodded at her.

They both went near the slender, long window and placed the the device to face it. Light rays beamed at the window, and it began to examine the earth. A tiny tablet hung upon the machine as well.

"There seem to have been more disappearances," said Femi, focusing on the tablet.

"Really?" asked Young-Chul.

Amelia nodded.

"Yes, there is."

"Femi, do you have the tablet?"

"Oh, yes, I do," replied Femi as he took it out at once from his bag.

Amelia took the tablet and opened an app.

"Okay, I will start noting things down, and then we can send our information to the station."

Femi again focused his eye.

"Global warming has increased to 20 per cent; sea level has risen 230 feet above the ground."

The astronauts looked toward the tablet. They could see the earth's statistics as it had black smoke forming around the earth. Femi continued.

"It has now impacted two more islands — the Grand Cayman in the Caribbean Sea and Capri in Italy."

As Femi said this, all the members once again looked over to the tablet and caught a glimpse of the destroyed Grand Cayman. The island was gone — it had disappeared. The greyish-black water had taken over the island, and it looked nothing like before. Capri in Italy was also in the same stage.

"Forests, notably the Amazon Forest that spans eight countries, is seeing increased temperatures and will soon face destruction. Ice caps and glaciers on the mountains of Antarctica and Greenland are melting. This water will quickly take over more islands."

The machine again showed mountains melting and water oozing out of them. Its beauty had long dissipated.

"Moreover, the loss of sea ice is getting accelerated, and the sea level is rising. As a result, there will be more intense heat waves."

"The surface of the earth is getting hotter by 40 per cent."

Femi had noted down the speech.

"That's it?" asked Vera, looking confused

"I think there's already too much — no, wait, there's more."

Amelia looked happy as she returned to her note-making.

The other members were staring at them and listening.

"Okay, guys — we need to check off things on our lists, remember? So, let's not disturb Femi and Amelia," said Young- Chul.

The other members returned to their work while Femi continued talking.

"Tropical storms have decreased by 9 per cent. However, snowfall and other severe hurricanes have also increased in a few countries — Afghanistan, Australia, Bengal — sorry, I meant Bangladesh, China, Denmark and Greece. Meanwhile, floods and droughts are also on the rise."

"And then we come to the study of planets in the solar system — astronauts are again visiting Mars from NASA, just as they had in the 2040s. Members of the Mars Team will give further information from their rockets."

Femi once again noted down his speech.

"Okay, that's good; I will send it to NASA."

Femi and Amelia put their devices back into their bags; Amelia was still holding on to her tablet.

The other members were still checking off things on the lists. Jacob and Idhant were on the front system talking with the chief. The TSRS had also contacted them the previous day as well as that morning. Dr Sanghvi checked to ensure that all their medicinal packages were in place, while Young-Chul and Vera checked the software uploaded in the rocket. The others were continuing the rest of the work. Jacob and Idhant were still talking to the chief.

"Yeah, and Femi and Amelia are completing their bonus tasks," said Idhant

"I see," said the chief on the other end. "Okay, guys- I need to go — I have a meeting. All of you, be careful and continue with your tasks, all right?"

Both astronauts nodded and said their farewell.

"My neck hurts — oh god," exclaimed Arham.

Everyone had taken off their helmets that morning — it was not compulsory to always wear the helmet. They needed some breathing room.

Arham leaned his head against the wall but accidentally hit his head on the heater of the missile.

"OUCH!"

Vera cracked a smile.

"Who told you to lean against the wall?" asked Vera.

"My neck hurts, all, right?" said Arham, irritated.

"He's an old man!" said Femi, laughing from the back.

Everyone laughed.

"I am 29! How is that old?" said Arham. He was taken aback by the fact that anyone could call him an old man.

Arham was, in fact, the youngest astronaut amongst the members. The TSRS had had no choice but to send someone so young due to logistical issues. However, they couldn't see why the station hadn't sent a more experienced astronaut who was good at technical piloting.

Chapter 17

"OUR FEARS ARE CONFIRMED."

Three weeks to go. On the second day of their mission, work began to pick up. Things were getting more hectic than anticipated. They needed to check off hundreds of lists, complete additional tasks, and take care of the enclosures. It all seemed very exhausting. Nevertheless, they didn't want the work to roll over to the next week. On 4 March, they were well and truly into their second week. At 5 pm, the chief contacted them once again. The call came up-front at the central system room where all the astronaut's seats were.

"Hey. Good afternoon to all," said chief Yohan, smiling slightly. This was unexpected. The chief had never been known to smile without reason.

"Good afternoon," everyone said in unison.

"Well — uh — how are your tasks going? Everything all right?"

"Yes," replied Idhant, sitting in the chair next to Jacob.

"Great!"

Suddenly, the chief looked startled and turned his attention to someone else close to him. The astronauts glanced at the chief curiously. Before long, a girl came and stood next to Yohan on the screen. Raima!

"Oh, hi!" exclaimed Raima, as she waved at the astronauts.

All of them waved at her and smiled.

"Finished your breakfast?" Yohan asked Raima.

Raima nodded. A lady called out Raima's name in the background.

Raima immediately left the room.

The astronauts turned to the back and gazed at the robot, who was checking off items on a list. Then, they all turned back to face the system.

"Yeah, you may have not noticed because you were all busy with work. Anyway, Young-Chul and Jacob had notified me that this was happening."

"And speaking of Young-Chul, I would like to talk to you privately.

"Me?" asked Young-Chul. "Sure."

"Yes, I thought it would be better to talk to the captain alone instead of everyone at once. Otherwise, I will eat into the other astronauts' schedules as well. Young-Chul can convey my message to you all later," said the chief.

Everyone nodded, but they were bewildered at why he wanted to speak to only Young-Chul. The chief had usually called them together if there was an issue.

"Young-Chul, you can move to the conference room. I will be switching the call to the line there," said the chief. Then, he turned to the rest of the astronauts.

"Yes, and the rest of you can continue your work. Please contact me again at night."

"Yeah, we will," said Jacob.

Young-Chul walked towards the conference room, which only took a few seconds; the room was near the food bay. He opened the door to the conference room and shut it quickly. The projector stood there with the chief's face fixed on Young-Chul.

"Young-Chul," the chief started directly.

"Yes, chief? What's the matter?" asked Young-Chul, who sat on one of the seats in the room.

"Well, you already know about the recordings, so there's no need to beat about the bush. We've been coming across more and more such items, and are all getting more and more worried by the second." The chief halted and again started talking.

"The most obvious thing for you to do is lead your members to the right path — in case anything happens on the planet, you should tell them about this matter."

"Of course," replied Young-Chul.

"I wanted to tell you something. This may come as a shock to you, but Barfee, our scientist…we-we just thought we would check the data on the planet again, and —"

The chief again halted. Young-Chul couldn't see why Yohan was having such difficulty articulating the problem.

"We have verified that there are living organisms on the planet."

Young-Chul's mouth flew wide open his mouth in surprise. He had foreseen that this might happen; his fears were confirmed now.

"But — we don't possibly know what kind of organism that is. It could be an animal or anything else. I don't think they could be human beings. Oh no, that would be horrendous — no."

Young-Chul tried to set his face as if he wasn't shaken.

"I see. Well, it's okay!" said Young-Chul trying to smile, but he couldn't. "I will make sure that all the team members are in a secure position, and —"

Young Chul recalled that he had something to ask the chief.

"Are these organisms all over Tian?"

" So far, we have only witnessed a few, and our computers won't be able search further too soon. That could take up a whole week as we try to alter the computations and programme it to search elsewhere on the planet" said the chief, looking anxious and uneasy. "In other words, I will inform you if we find something else."

"Okay, chief. Should I tell the others about this —"

"No-No!" said the chief exclaiming a little bit. "Oh, sorry, Young-Chul, well — no — you shouldn't tell them about this matter, but if something comes up, you can notify them, like I said."

"I understand, chief. Could you tell me what I should inform them about from this meeting?"

"Yes, tell them that Tian is getting a little superheated — I will send you the statistics. You should all be wearing the extra spacesuits we gave you, the thermal, insulated ones, three days before reaching the planet," said the chief.

"I will, chief," Young-Chul said with a slight smile. "Is there anything else you would like to tell me?"

" No, I don't think there is anything else to say. But, of course, you should take your meals on time and stay hydrated."

Young-Chul nodded.

" Thank you for cooperation, Young Chul. There's just one more week — do well."

Young-Chul nodded once again. The chief seemed very anxious; it was obvious that he was expecting something terrible to happen.

"Bye, tell Jacob to contact me for a group call at night."

"Yes, chief — we will be sure to do that. Bye," Young-Chul smiled.

Young-Chul cut the call and opened the door.

There was no one was at the front. He had been apprehensive at first, wondering if someone had overheard their conversation. Such a person would have been sure to think that he and the chief had betrayed the group. However, there was no one outside. Young-Chul was still shaken about the "living organisms". As he walked past the storage area, he saw Alf and Arham crossing things off their lists. He looked at them both. The two seemed to be in some sort of heated argument.

Alf was placing some tins on the table.

"Alf, you shouldn't be placing them there — you should place them on the shelf," said Arham.

"How many times?" groaned Arham

Arham turned around and saw Young-Chul.

"Oh — Captain!" said Arham, grinning. "You look tired this morning."

"I haven't been sleeping very well," said Young-Chul nervously, smiling.

"Well — the chief said he wanted you to share something," said Arham looking inquisitive.

"Yes — about that, Arham, let's discuss that with the others."

Arham turned to look over at Alf.

"Alf, make sure you put the things in their appropriate place, okay? Otherwise, it will go haywire here."

"Yes, of course," replied Alf.

Young-Chul somehow stopped himself from laughing and said: "Arham, it's okay, take it easy."

Young-Chul didn't know how to feel comfortable now. He felt guilty about not sharing this problem with the other members.

"Alf," said Young-Chul looking toward the robot.

"Yes, sir?" asked Alf looking hopefully towards Young-Chul.

"You can join us in our discussion — this is about the spacesuits."

"Of course, Thank you," said Alf looking gleeful.

"Wait," said Arham. "Does the robot need to wear a spacesuit?"

"Yes, when we reach Tian, Alf will need to. He doesn't need to wear it in the rocket, but he does need to on Tian."

" Oh. Riveting," replied Arham.

The three walked out of the storage area and to the system area.

Vera, who had immediately seen them, asked: "Is everything all right? What did the chief say?"

Everyone gathered around them.

"Yes, the chief just told me that Tian has been getting hotter, and we need to switch to our thermal spacesuits three days before we reach the planet."

"Oh, that's it?" asked Idhant. "Why did the meeting last so long, then?"

Young-Chul made up a quick excuse.

"He was explaining the statistics. He told us that he would send them to us. When he does so, I will send them over to Vera. Vera, please take a look when they arrive."

"Yes," said Vera, who still had the paper with all the information about Tian.

"Okay, I think we have finished checking off most items on the list, as well as finished our other work. Let's call it a break," said the captain.

Some of the astronauts had gone to their sleeping compartments while the others stayed back, lying in their seats.

Chapter 18

CK-321: THE ALIEN SPACESHIP

On the 17th of April, it was their final day of the mission. At 9 am, they would be able to disembark on the planet Tian. As soon as the astronauts woke up in their sleeping compartments, they realized that they were sweating; it was evident that they were closer to the planet. Their room was extensive, with many beds for each astronaut; it was spacious enough to fit 20 people there. Their morning routine went precisely as intended. They had all been wearing their thermal spacesuits for the previous three days. They started to get ready and eat breakfast. Alf was as happy as usual. According to the directions on the system, the rocket was moving on its own now, towards Tian.

Dr Sanghvi carried with him an electronic box which everyone assumed was filled with medical essentials. Vera brought along the map and a sheaf of papers that described Tian's statistics. Jacob and Idhant had taken charge of contacting the chief before their task started, and Arham handled the usual technical tools, ably assisted by Alf. Femi and Amelia couldn't be more occupied with the assignments they had been given by NASA — yet they were helping to whatever extent they could. Young-Chul stood in a corner collecting the small camera gadget everyone would be wearing... yet, in the midst of all that, he couldn't get the information about the living organisms out of his head. Would they encounter the creatures when they landed on Tian? He waved aside the thought and continued his work.

Amelia, who had finished her task, was walking towards the central system, and found Young-Chul lurking in the corner.

"Is everything going smoothly?"

Young-Chul turned to see her, and Amelia knew he had not seen that coming.

"Oh, yes. I am just collecting the cameras. Would you mind distributing them? I must go and give Alf a few instructions."

"Yeah, sure!" replied Amelia.

Amelia took the cameras and gathered everyone around to hand out the equipment.

Young-Chul had gone towards Alf, who was standing with Arham. He spent five minutes explaining things to Alf and making sure he understood.

"Yes, sir. I understand," replied Alf.

"Great. Let's all go to the main room. We need to get ready; it's almost 8 am."

Arham and Alf nodded and followed Young-Chul.

"Okay, everyone! "

The astronauts quickly turned their attention toward the captain and gathered around.

"Is everything okay? Nothing wrong with the rocket?"

"No. Nothing," replied Idhant and the others.

"Good. Have your cameras stuck to your spacesuits, and strap in all the necessities we need. It's almost 8 am, so we should take our seats."

"Jacob and Idhant, do the countdown as soon as you finish the system check."

They both nodded.

Everyone settled into their usual seats.

Jacob and Idhant took a few minutes to complete a thorough check.

Jacob yelled: "It's going to take us an hour to reach! The rocket will now speed up…in 3,2,1!"

The spacecraft propelled itself into thin air, and everyone held on to their seat handles. The rocket was going faster than it had ever done on this mission, and they had another hour to endure it. During this time, the astronauts had again leaned against their seats.

Soon, 30 minutes had gone by, and all the astronauts were becoming active. Everyone had their necessities, and everything was going just flawlessly.

While Arham leaned against his seat, the rocket shook for some time.

All the team members stared at Jacob and Idhant for an answer to what had just happened.

"Guys, it's nothing," replied Jacob.

"Yeah, it's probably the atmosphere around the planet. Such movement is normal because the temperatures are getting high," said Idhant.

Femi looked over to the glass window, staring into the gorgeous atmosphere. How wonderful it was. He couldn't help but smile a little — however, there was something in space that blocked a part of his vision.

It looked like a green object; he was certain that it was coming toward them.

"Captain?" asked Femi

"Yes?"

"I don't know whether it's just my window that is emitting some sort of green light, but you can see something outside — like some object."

Young-Chul immediately looked over to his window; he had also encountered the same thing. All the astronauts sitting in the same row as the captain looked out of their glass windows, but the others on the opposite side found it difficult to see anything. They leaned to the left to discern what was happening.

"Jacob, can you see it?" asked Young-Chul

"Yes, I can, but I know what you are going to ask, and I can tell you right now — I have no idea," replied Jacob.

"Wait, we should switch to the computer mode; it might help us," said Idhant calmly.

It seemed like a small matter, but they were all plagued by the same existential dread — they did not want to end up like the people on the last mission. What was the worst that could happen?

Jacob nodded and switched it on.

The computer replied: "Unknown celestial body — CK-321."

"CK-321?" asked Vera

"Is that the name of a spacecraft?"

Vera had asked the worst possible question that would be answered in just a few seconds.

Young-Chul was confused; could it be related to the living organism?

Suddenly, a loud screeching voice travelled through their spacecraft, and everyone clapped their hands to their helmets in horror. The sound was transmitting over the radio and all the wires on their spacecraft. It continued for a few seconds and stopped.

They all gazed into each other's faces, knowing that none of them would know the answer to this. Young-Chul was surprised — this was the same sound he had heard on the recording! He knew what he had to do.

"Guys — I need to tell you something. The —" Young Chul was unluckily interrupted by a call from the chief. Jacob picked it up immediately.

"Hey everyone, is the mission going —"

"Sir!" exclaimed Young-Chul

The chief raised his eyebrows, confused.

"There's a loud screeching noise around our spacecraft and an object outside. Is that normal?" asked Dr Sanghvi, terrified.

Everyone knew that this was definitely not normal but still hoped the chief would answer adequately.

"What do you mean, nothing —"

The loud screeching voice sounded once again, and the chief also shut his ears as he heard it. His eyes widened, and Young-Chul knew immediately that Yohan had realised what it was.

The chief looked horror-struck.

"Okay, here's what we do — we will immediately check into what that is. Don't hang up the call."

Everyone nodded.

But the call started glitching, and the screeching voice was getting even louder over the next two minutes. Before they knew it, the call had disconnected. Then, unexpectedly, Alf and Young-Chul stood up and went to the system. Young-Chul started clicking buttons to steer the ship away from the other "CK-321" spacecraft. Alf, however, was scanning all the computers to find any information that could save them.

However, to everyone's surprise, even as Young-Chul throttled the system aggressively, the missile was only pushed towards the direction of the other spacecraft. It was as if some magnetic force was pulling them towards the other rocket. Their rocket now started moving about so violently that no one could get up from their seats. Young-Chul and Alf almost fell over but clung to Jacob and Idhant's seat handles. The light of the Ck-321 spacecraft grew brighter and brighter, and their rocket began to inch even closer to the other one. Everyone grew more and more terrified as they felt the uncontrollable magnetic attraction. There was nothing they could do now. Young-Chul and Alf fell to the floor while the others slumped against their seats, unconscious.

Chapter 19

THERE IS LIFE ON TIAN

The rocket was filled with gas as a group of slender, greenish people entered it. As the people looked around, they could see the astronauts lying down, still unconscious. Then, finally, one of the new entrants turned back to one of his companions and flashed him a "You know what to do" look. The rocket was speeding as fast as ever — it was going to land on Tian. But unfortunately, the greenish beings were still on the rocket, not even bothering to help. The rocket thudded to a halt as it landed on Tian. The glass windows of the rocket broke into innumerable splinters.

Idhant's eyes were blurry — all he could see was red. He thought someone had put chillies in his eyes. He slowly woke up, thinking that he had fainted while on the rocket.

"Captain?" asked Idhant in a raspy and slow voice.

Idhant turned to look at the ground and realised he wasn't sitting inside the rocket anymore: he was sitting atop a mound of red sand. He turned to look this way and that — red sand everywhere. He pinched his arms, thinking that he must be dreaming. He again turned to look forward to see if there was anything beyond the sand and this time, he saw a thin, greenish body standing in front of him, with round, wide white eyes.

Idhant shrieked a bit, leapt, and pushed himself backwards. The creature gave him a look that Idhant thought looked like a smirk. But the beast wasn't alone; the others seemed to be his friends.

The other astronauts also woke up slowly and turned to look at the beasts. They shrieked even louder than Idhant and quickly pushed themselves up to standing.

"What's happening? Where are we?" asked Vera, horrified.

Everyone felt utter perplexity and confusion.

Young-Chul tried to recollect what he could: all he could remember was that there had been a problem with the rocket, and he had fallen unconscious; what had happened next? How had they reached this greenish looking world?

The greenish people took a step towards the astronauts.

"STAY BACK!" yelled Young-Chul

He had realised that none of them were carrying their weapons; all they had were electric tools. He remembered that Alf had a weapon, however, and he quickly grabbed an electric weapon from the robot's hand.

The beasts gave what sounded like a laugh.

Standing at the front, their leader said something strange that no one could understand: "Yu oust marque da water?"

Alf widened his robotic eyes and turned to his members.

"He's asking us whether we had planned to take water from here," said Alf

Everyone gasped in surprise.

Young-Chul realised how this had happened and told his members.

"The robot has remarkable linguistic abilities installed in its frame. It can translate any language."

"What language is this? How did we even land here?" whispered Femi to Young-Chul.

Young-Chul once again realised what they were dealing with. Maybe this was the living organism. Perhaps this was Tian.

The leader spoke again: "Yu nez do ezga."

Everyone looked toward Alf.

"He is saying that we haven't answered their question yet."

Young-Chul thought for a while and decided to be honest. What if they could tell that the astronauts had lied?

"Tell them yes," replied Young-Chul to Alf.

"WHAT?" whispered Arham. "WE DON'T EVEN KNOW WHAT THEY ARE!"

Young-Chul decided to wave aside the problem and nodded at Alf for him to answer the creature.

Alf replied: "Yequeste."

The creatures looked at one another.

Their leader said something to his companions.

Suddenly, the astronauts and Alf fell unconscious.

They again woke up — this time, on the floor. Around them was a chamber of metal — with no one around. There were grey bricks fixed into the walls and a table in front of them; both the walls and the table had words written on them in some sort of unknown language.

They all stood in the same place, not knowing what to do. Finally, Young-Chul looked towards the device held around his arm and tried to contact the chief. However, he couldn't, no matter how hard he tried.

"I cannot contact him either," said Idhant, disappointed.

Young-Chul let out an angry sigh and turned toward the others.

"I want to tell you something."

"I don't know what it is, Captain, but I don't think now is the time for any divulgences. We are stuck in a place and have no way of getting out."

"Yes, but this is important! I'd better tell you now before those creatures come."

Without letting anyone else speak, Young-Chul started talking. He explained everything he had heard on the recordings and what the chief had told him during that night when the TSRS had confirmed the existence of an unknown living organism. After he had finished explaining, he turned to look around at the others. They didn't look very happy.

"I don't want to blame you for anything," said Femi. "The chief only told you to hide it from us."

"But why would he do that? Doesn't he trust us?" asked Vera.

" Look," said Arham. "That's not the point! We have to focus on getting ourselves the water, and before that, figure out a way to deal with these creatures."

"Okay," replied Young-Chul. "Half of you can go to that side," continued Young-Chul, pointing to one of the brick doors that was closed shut.

"Try and open that with our tools. The rest of you can help me with this door."

There were two doors in that room, and Young-Chul, Idhant, Dr Sanghvi and Arham went to one door while the others went to the other.

They tried to break it open using the electrical tools that they had luckily stored in the pockets of their spacesuits. But nothing worked. No matter how advanced the citizens of earth were, they were clearly less so than the citizens of Tian.

Nevertheless, they tried for 30 minutes. The creatures had not yet come, and they were worried about whether they could get out in time.

Vera looked here and there, and then, suddenly, discovered that there was another door — on the other side, stood a group of people, staring at them and knocking hard on the door.

Chapter 20

GRETE AND WATER ON TIAN

Vera managed to hold back a scream and called out to Young-Chul.

"Captain?"

"Yes?" Young-Chul looked extremely tired but wanted to attend to Vera's question.

Vera pointed to the door behind which stood the group of people, still knocking.

Young-Chul had widened his eyes, and so did the others. He had recognised one of the people outside the door — Aveen! These were the people from the previous mission, who had come here to find water! Everyone had realised who these people were, and they now went immediately towards the door.

"WAIT!" yelled Idhant

"Are you sure that the creatures are not trying to trick us?"

Everyone thought for a while.

"No," replied Young-Chul. "We need to help them."

The others proceeded to follow him, as did Idhant.

They tried to break open the door, but it didn't work.

Suddenly, the door from the other side opened, revealing the creatures again.

"What do you want? Let us out of here!" yelled Jacob.

These creatures were not the leader and his companions who had imprisoned them. This was a much older greenish man.

"Now, we are not holding you as prisoners," said the creature.

To everyone's surprise, the creature could speak English.

"I assume that you have come here on the orders of your space station in search of water. But we can't give you water."

"Why?" asked Femi

"It is our water. We know that you do not have water on earth. So, what I can tell you is, that you shall be stuck here on our planet until you are able to give us something precious in return. If you can do so, you are free to leave with our water."

The astronauts thought for a while but couldn't think of anything precious to give.

"The other group of astronauts from 2045 are also stuck here. They had also come here searching for water but didn't have anything precious to offer in exchange."

"Come along with us; we shall show you how our water is made."

The astronauts scanned each other's faces, and Young-Chul nodded at them. They could do nothing now as Tian's citizens were more powerful than them.

"But, what about them?" asked Young-Chul to the old man-creature, pointing at the other group of astronauts.

The creature laughed.

"Oh! They are just having their lunch. They might be eager to meet you. But you must do so only after you have come with us."

The older man's companions went toward the astronauts and held them by their hands, forcing them to walk ahead.

They all walked forward and outside the room. The creatures had filled the whole place with greyish-black bricks — it seemed to be a mansion full of unknown objects they had never seen before.

They soon walked out of the house and saw land. The land looked beautiful. There was sunrise and plenty of colourful homes and many buildings and factories. Yet, it looked nothing like earth.

"Beautiful, isn't it?" said the old man to the captain.

"Who are you?" asked Young-Chul.

"Me?" said the old man and laughed. "I am the president of this world, or you call it, Tian!"

"Perhaps a more precise question would be, WHAT ARE YOU!" yelled Arham. All the astronauts glared at Arham at this sudden outburst. Who knows what would happen?

"You may call us — aliens."

Everyone was shocked, as if realising their childhood dreams had come true.

"Let's move forward."

They walked through the reddish sand and towards one of the factories nearby. The older man decided to take an electric bolt car to reach there. The car was in the shape of a circle which was big enough to fit 30 people, and it was powered by electricity. So, they all sat in their seats comfortably. After a few minutes of riding in the vast car, they got down only to see a massive factory. It was made up of glass windows and covered in blue paint.

Through the windows, everyone could see several aliens sitting and working.

"Come in with us; this is our largest water factory here," said the old man.

They walked up the brick-shaped stairs and into the building. There were several aliens walking around, carrying boards, talking to one another. One of the aliens working as the receptionist walked towards the older man.

"Maquesta! Hascvy equs na ze!"

"Ye," replied the older man.

"Gracq, eq yu to me."

The older man nodded and gestured to everyone to follow him. They walked towards the electric elevator, which was huge; the older man's companions were still holding on to the astronauts as if they the latter were here to rob them.

The elevator reached the fourth floor — they could make out it out as it was the only sign written in English.

The elevator door opened, revealing a vast glass tank of water with several aliens checking its systems. All the astronauts and Alf gasped in surprise.

"Just wonderful," the older man spoke and snickered.

They walked towards the tank, which was about eight feet long. It was transparent, and a tremendous amount of water flowed through it.

"This water comes from our seas and oceans!"

"There are seas and oceans here?" asked Young-Chul weakly. Enough surprises had happened today — first, they had met the aliens, then, their friends and now, this.

"Yes," replied the older man. "There's more."

Next to the water tank stood a large stone stand that all the astronauts assumed was liquid that the machine was producing.

"Sir?" asked Amelia. The older man looked at her.

"What does that machine produce?"

"Water!" said the older man, once again chuckling.

"May I ask you your name?" asked Young-Chul.

"My name? Grete!"

"Grete?' asked Young-Chul.

Grete nodded.

Young-Chul flashed Grete his usual smile and asked him one more question.

"How do you make your water?

"Ah-ha!" yelled Grete making everyone jump.

"That I won't tell you!"

"Sir," said Dr Sanghvi.

"Call me Grete."

"Grete, we understand that you want to show us your production of water. But our earth needs it — and we need to go back immediately, with the previous mission's astronauts."

"Now — now," said Grete, looking slightly angry. "If you do that, you and your other people won't be able to learn a lesson! You and your people have made a mess of your world and have created this suffering for yourselves! You are the ones who have destroyed your own homes! You have destroyed your water, trees, animals — everything!"

The astronauts were speechless; they didn't know what to say.

"Let's leave the matter," said Grete. "I will take you back to your house now."

"House?" said Arham. "We are not living here."

"You don't have anything precious to give, so, yes, you are indeed living here as prisoners."

All the astronauts and Alf were terrified. This was a terrible day.

Chapter 21

THE REUNION OF
THE ASTRONAUTS

They went into the elevator and walked out of the building. It was already night, and it seemed to have come much sooner than expected. They went through the electric bolt car again and reached their so-called "house". As soon as they got off the electric bolt car, they saw the outer facade of their house — it was a stunning yellow mansion. They walked into the house and into what was their "prisoner room".

"You can meet the others," said Grete. Grete and his comrades left, leaving the new astronauts and the previous mission's astronauts alone.

Alf and the astronauts went to where all the previous mission's members were sitting. It looked like they were waiting for them. Fortunately, now the door was open between the two sets of astronauts. They all went and hugged each other.

"What happened to you all! How did you end up here?" asked Young-Chul to Aveen. Aveen was the captain of the previous mission.

"We were hit by the alien's spacecraft, and we couldn't get out of here!" said Aveen. "How are you all? How is everyone back on earth? What about the TSRS? We haven't been able to contact them since!"

Young-Chul didn't know how he could answer all of Aveen's queries at once.

"We are okay, everyone back on earth — well, the problem has gotten worse. That's why they sent us here! The chief —"

"Yohan?" asked Aveen.

"Yeah, him. We couldn't contact him either!"

"Nice robot you have here," said Aveen looking towards Alf, standing next to Young-Chul.

On the other side, the rest of the astronauts talked to each other. All of them were very glad to see their friends alive.

"What about Ira?" asked Kiara to Dr Sanghvi.

"She's fine, don't worry! Hopefully, we can find a way out of here."

Nihaan, Sidharth, Sean, Dr Abridhanta and Naaz from the previous mission were still talking with the rest of the members — some of them were almost in tears, asking the new batch endless questions. They had spent the past five years on Tian, not able to contact earth ever since.

"Guys!" yelled Young-Chul at everyone.

All the astronauts quickly turned toward him.

"I know that this reunion is wonderful — it's incredible to see everyone, but now we need to find a way out of here!"

Everyone nodded.

"But we don't have anything precious to give!" exclaimed Aveen. "What are we going to do?"

For a while, both the captains, Aveen and Young-Chul, thought for a while, and Aveen said: "Let's all discuss this. Maybe we could join up the chairs and place them near that table."

Aveen pointed at the table inside the MN-04 team's prisoner room.

They all carried chairs from both rooms and joined them up together near the table. They then sat around the table, looking at one another. It took a few minutes for them to settle in as 16 people had to squeeze in together, making room for one another. Once they had finished adjusting, Young-Chul spoke.

"Okay- — uh — Aveen."

"Yes?" asked Aveen

"Is your spacecraft still on Tian?"

"No," replied Aveen

"Why not? We saw ours, while we went to the water factory."

"Well — you see", began Aveen, sounding like he was about to tell them a story. "Once we crashed onto Tian, they locked us up. We tried many different things, such as running out of the prisoner house to reach our spacecraft. But nothing would work. Finally, in order to deter us from trying anything else, they destroyed our spacecraft."

"WHAT?" asked Femi

"Yeah."

"But will they do the same thing to ours?" asked Amelia, looking terrified.

"I don't think so — if you don't make any ruckus, that might not happen," replied Sidharth.

"Okay, so we should not make any ruckus — and that includes you, Arham!" said Young-Chul.

Arham looked grumpy and sat straight in his seat.

"So," began Young-Chul. "Since you all don't have yours," he said, looking towards Aveen. "And we have ours, there must be something we could give to them."

"Yeah," said Dr Abridhanta in agreement. "There might be some things the aliens don't know about."

Young-Chul nodded.

Everyone thought for a while.

"What about wires?" asked Amelia.

"Amelia, I think they already have wires — otherwise, they wouldn't be able to conduct electricity," replied Idhant.

"Right," said Amelia.

"Camera?" asked Sean Nigam from the other team.

Everyone shook their heads.

"No, they already have that," said Aveen

No matter how hard they thought, nothing "precious" could come to their minds.

"Guys, it's already 10."

"What?" exclaimed Arham. "Why does the time go so fast here?"

"That's the way Tian works," said Kiara.

"Yes," replied Young-Chul. "We should sleep now. We can get up early in the morning to discuss this further."

Everyone nodded and got up from their seats.

"Wait —" said Jacob, causing everyone to turn and look towards him.

"So — where do we sleep then? On the floor? I am just asking — not that I can't adjust to sleeping on the floor."

"No-no — there's a separate bunker bedroom," said Kiara.

"There is?" asked Idhant, looking awestruck.

"Yeah," replied Kiara.

She opened the door, and everyone could see a bunch of bunker beds placed neatly — it was perfect.

"Thanks," said Jacob.

Kiara smiled.

"Wait — so where are you all going to sleep then?" Young-Chul asked Aveen.

"We all need to sleep in the same room. There's only one room with these bunker beds."

"Oh right," said Young-Chul

They all bade each other goodnight. All the astronauts had removed their spacesuits and now went to sleep in their regular clothes underneath the suits. The astronauts and the robot needed to execute a plan tomorrow — to get themselves out of Tian with water in tow.

Chapter 22

THE BREAK-IN

Jacob woke up to a sunny morning, the sharp rays hitting his eyes. The bunker beds were close to windows through which the light was filtering in and piercing his eyes. Jacob reached out in disgruntlement, trying to reach out to Sean whose bed was right next to him, and accidentally pressed a button on the wall.

Immediately, all the astronauts woke up as an alarming sound blasted around the room — causing everyone to put their hands around their ears. The disturbing sound stopped at once, and suddenly the room's wooden door opened. It was the aliens. Everyone's eyes flew open, as they realised it hadn't been the aliens who had made the alarming sound.

One of the aliens took a step forward, and once again, all the astronauts assumed that he was the leader.

"Maquesta yu ina swqu?" said the alien leader.

One of the leader's comrades slapped him on his back, and the leader yelled in pain.

"NAFASA!"

The leader and his companion were arguing about something and now, they turned their attention toward the astronauts.

"Did any of you turn on the alarm button?" said the leader. To everyone's horror, this alien could also speak English.

"YOU CAN SPEAK ENGLISH AS —?" said Arham, who was quickly interrupted by Idhant putting his hands around Arham's mouth to shush him. Meanwhile, Jacob spoke up while Arham tried to prise Idhant's hands off his mouth.

"I am genuinely sorry. While I was trying to reach out to one of my friends, I accidentally clicked the button. I wasn't aware that there was such a thing. I am very sorry."

Everyone glared at him. They hadn't expected Jacob to do such a thing.

The aliens looked toward him in pregnant silence. They thought that Jacob was acting suspiciously.

"All right. Please be careful not to touch the button again." said the alien leader.

Jacob nodded. The aliens left at once, leaving everyone confused.

"YOU TOUCHED THE BUTTON?" said Femi, looking awestruck.

"Yes, I am sorry for waking you all up."

"It's okay," said Young-Chul and Aveen in unison. First, both astronauts glared at each other. Then, everyone started to glare at them as well. It seemed like they both had communicated telepathically.

"Wow," began Dr Sanghvi, who was sleeping in a corner on her bed. "Jacob's being clumsy for the first time in his life."

Everyone let out a giggle.

"What's the time?" asked Sidharth.

"Wait," said Aveen looking towards the device held around his hand.

"It's 2 am on earth."

"What's the time on Tian?" asked Sidharth.

"6 am."

"I think it's a good time to start our discussion."

Everyone nodded.

"Wait, isn't there a bathroom around where we can brush and stuff like that?" asked Arham, who was still angry about Idhant.

"Yeah, of course," said Aveen pointing to a corner of the room where there were two bathrooms.

"The women can go to the bathroom on the left, while the men can go to the other side."

"Okay," said Young-Chul. "I need everyone to get ready in at least 20 minutes."

Everyone rushed towards the bathrooms, one by one, and each person took their turn. After they had finished using the toilet, everyone wore their spacesuits once again; Tian was getting hotter but luckily, everyone had their thermal spacesuits.

They went to the table and once again sat in their seats.

"Does anyone have any ideas about what we can give to the aliens?"

Everyone shook their heads.

"I tried to think about it," began Femi. "But nothing good would come to my mind."

Everyone nodded in agreement.

Young-Chul had spent half the time in his bunker bed, lying awake and thinking about it.

"I don't know whether this is important or not..." began Sean.

"What is it?" asked Aveen.

"It's about the system in that water factory."

"You went there as well?" asked Young-Chul

Aveen nodded.

"They also wanted to offer us this so-called lesson about water."

"I see. Well, Sean. What did you want to tell us?"

"When we went there — to the factory — I happened to see some kind of security room near a corner."

"And?" asked Young-Chul

"Well, it might contain some high-level security system. I caught a glimpse and could see that it was a contact centre — the aliens probably use it to contact outer space."

Young Chul widened his eyes.

"Are you sure?"

"Yeah."

"Young-Chul — you see — Sean is also an expert technical pilot, so what he is saying must be correct."

Young-Chul nodded and spoke: "But it's not like we can contact anyone from there. We can't just, like, break into the room, can we?"

"That's exactly what I thought," said Sean, looking uncomfortable.

Sean continued.

"Look — Grete made us go to that water factory a lot of times, to see the water, and I have noticed that during a particular time the aliens take a break, exit the room and do some other tasks. After about 30 minutes, they come in again."

Everyone froze.

"So, are you telling us that we should go into that room when the aliens temporarily exit and try to contact the TSRS?" asked Aveen, sure that he was joking.

"Yes."

"Sean, as much as I would like to get out of here, I am not sure about this. It's just not the right to, do you know?" said Young-Chul, looking more uncomfortable than ever.

"Yes, yes, I know, Young-Chul," said Sean. "But we have spent five years here, and you guys have only come here like yesterday. We have had a lot of time to despair."

"I guess it might work. Let's give it a try?"

Everyone scrutinised the others carefully, particularly trying to read Young-Chul and Aveen's minds. But, again, they seemed to be communicating only telepathically.

Young-Chul thought this might work.

"Should we give it a try then?" he asked Aveen

"Maybe we should. We should probably take some risk now."

Young-Chul nodded.

"Is everyone okay with this plan?" asked Young-Chul looking at all the astronauts, who seemed more confident since their captains had articulated that this would be a good plan.

"I think it's good," said Femi. "But will it work?"

"We will see. Now, we should discuss how to get inside."

Everyone nodded and sat closer to the table to hear Sean's plan.

Sean was talking about the timings, how to get inside, et al — and it seemed like a perfect plan.

"But will Grete take us to the water factory?" asked Kiara.

"Yes, they should. Grete might say that there are more things to see in the water factory."

"Good. Is everyone on board with the plan? No objections?" asked Aveen.

Fortunately, everyone was on board. It was wonderful to have a team that cooperated with them.

"Breakfast will come any time now," said Dr Abridhanta.

They all waited for some time, and as expected, the door opened with three aliens walking inside, with plates loaded on electric trays floating in mid-air. The food was, luckily, human food. There were pieces of toast with jam and a few fried pappads for them. Everyone ate their food hungrily. The aliens placed the plates on the electric tray again, once the astronauts and Alf had eaten.

Alf seemed very distant. He kept quiet but joined in occasionally, to discuss a few ideas about the "break-in".

Grete suddenly walked into the room.

"I see you have already reunited. I need to take the present team back again to the water factory. There's more to see!"

The MN-04 team nodded. The previous mission members were left behind; they all flashed smiles toward their other friends, wishing them good luck to get to the room.

The MN-04 team was prepared for what was to come as they walked out of their prisoner's house. They again took an electric bolt car to the same water factory and went inside the building.

It had stayed the same — packed with aliens walking around holding papers. They could see the call centre office with words written on a board above it, in the alien language, as they walked by. This was the room they were targeting to contact the TSRS.

Grete and the astronauts went through the same elevator to the fourth floor. There were more. They had already seen the massive tank and the machine producing water. Now, Grete wanted to show them a highly sophisticated map of the whole of Tian. He was telling them about the history of Tian and its seas and oceans and, to everyone's disinterest, about how Tian was able to survive with the help of people who always loved Tian and wanted to do their best for their home. While Grete explained everything, Idhant had to put up his best act.

"Grete?" asked Idhant.

"Yes?"

"Could I go to the bathroom?"

"Sure-um — let one of the aliens take you there."

"Thank you," said Idhant.

One of the aliens held Idhant by his hand and forcefully took him towards the bathroom on the same floor. The alien stood outside, and Idhant entered the bathroom.

"I also need to drink water so it might take some time," said Idhant. The alien nodded.

But this was just the beginning of the plan. Idhant entered one of the cubicles and took out his electric tool. Then, quietly, he raised his tool towards an electric vent just on top of him. He unscrewed it and jumped up, slipping inside the vent. Luckily, the vent was at the perfect height for Idhant to jump to. He closed the vent door again and squished through the cubical metal box. He had to crawl through it to get to the room. He crawled for some time, quickly, as he knew he had to be fast. As expected, he reached the vent door leading into the room. He opened it using the same tool and jumped downwards.

The aliens had filled the room with computers, and Idhant quickly sat in one of the seats. Luckily, the laptop was already on. He clicked on a few buttons making the computer contact the outside space. It was extraordinary. There was an option to reach earth as well as a specific place.

He typed to the coordinates for TSRS, Earth. The computer started glitching and a voice sounded, but it wasn't clear.

Chapter 23

NO SUCH LUCK

The sound wasn't audible. No matter how hard Idhant tried adjusting it, he couldn't set it to the right frequency. Immediately, a sound also occurred behind the door. The aliens were coming back. But it was unexpected as the astronauts had thought that they would typically come after 30 minutes. He couldn't contact the TSRS now. What could he do? He could try and send the link over to their spacecraft so that, when they got a chance, they could access it or jump back to the vent and team up with the rest of the astronauts. Idhant was still trying to decide when the aliens started to come over. Suddenly, Idhant's device strapped to his arm, flickered. It was a call from Sean — Idhant picked it up.

"GET OUT OF THERE RIGHT NOW!"

Idhant didn't need to be told twice. He cut the call.

He had to get back to the vent. He erased the website's memory, jumped back into the vent, and closed the door. He looked through the narrow spaces between the vent door to see if the aliens had arrived. They had. Four aliens had entered without even noticing anything. Idhant quickly crawled back into the bathroom, which only took him seconds. He jumped back and pretended to flush the toilet. He came out of the bathroom and saw that the alien was still standing there, with a poker face.

"Sorry, I took some time."

The alien walked away towards the elevator, and Idhant began following him. Finally, they reached the fourth floor again — to see Grete still talking to the astronauts. They had noticed Idhant at once but decided not to ask him anything yet. If they did, the aliens might get suspicious.

Grete explained for some more time until it was noon.

"Okay," said Grete. "I think we can all go back to your house now."

They all left in the same electric bolt car towards their house without another word. They entered their prisoner's house and went inside their room.

The previous mission's members were still waiting for them.

"Did you get to contact the TSRS?" asked Nihaan curiously.

"Yeah, we wanted to ask you too, but Grete was there," said Young-Chul.

"I am sorry," said Idhant. Everyone assumed that he had failed once they heard this.

"I did try to contact the TSRS. But all that came through was a glitch. It wasn't audible, no matter how hard I tried to adjust it. The aliens too foiled our plans. They arrived way earlier than I thought."

"They did?" asked Dr Sanghvi.

"Yeah. The aliens arrived just after two minutes."

"WHAT? But Sean —" said Kiara. "You said they would come after 30 minutes."

"I- I thought they would. That's what they usually do," said Sean.

"Anyway," said Young-Chul. "We should be able to contact the TSRS the next time we try."

"But did the aliens notice anything?"

"No," said Idhant. "They didn't."

"That's a relief."

"The aliens served us lunch for both of our teams," said Aveen. "We thought we would wait until you returned."

"You shouldn't have done that," said Amelia.

They all sat and ate the tasty meal. It was a green salad and it was mouthwatering — even better than earth's space food. There were lot of tasty ingredients in the salad, even though the astronauts couldn't identify any of them. Naaz finished her lunch first and went to the bathroom to wash her hands. Nihaan from the previous mission team was still thinking about what they could give to the aliens. He was struggling with possibilities in his mind.

"A camera?"

"No, no — that wouldn't work."

"A cellphone."

"Aliens are already very technologically advanced."

Nihaan thought for a while and then, had a brainwave.

"Mangoes? Wait."

"Mangoes. That can work!"

Suddenly, out of the blue, Nihaan yelled out: "Mangoes!"

Chapter 24

ASTRONAUTS ARE ALIVE

Once again, the Thumba Space Research Station in Kerala had become the centre of all news worldwide. TSRS expressed great confidence when speaking to the media that their astronauts would come back — but they didn't feel as confident since they had heard the call on their spacecraft die. The chief was in utmost depression. Nothing would work, no matter how much anyone tried to give him some hope. The scientists at the TSRS tried their very best, and they were still trying to find the MN-04 team. The chief was swivelling around in his computer chair and pacing around his office. Suddenly, he heard a notification on his tab as a Newslet newsletter popped up. He swiped up to see the info.

"TSRS: Are the astronauts on board?"

The past few weeks have given us the most exclusive news of this decade! As our readers will recall, the famous TSRS sent a group of astronauts to the planet Tian. The chief had confirmed in the early stages of the mission that everything was going quite well. However, the TSRS have stopped giving out any information about the team in the past couple of days. Read on for a conversation between a Newslet reporter and a scientist from the KKS space station in Kozhikode, Kerala.

'Have you kept abreast of the strange goings on in the TSRS?'

'Yes, I have been reading about it.'

'And what might you say about the problem that seems to be brewing?'

'I do agree with the people on earth. TSRS has voluntarily stopped giving information about Tian and its MN-04 team — that, in my opinion, is a sign of something having gone wrong, very violently wrong. Only that could explain why have stopped giving people info. According to a few scientists at the KKS, the MN-04 team might have crashed somewhere near Tian. This might be predicated on the fact that the TSRS stopped giving information on the same day that the spacecraft was scheduled to land on Tian. Every scientist, including me, has the right to voice their opinion. We've been successful on almost all erstwhile space missions!'

'Yes, sir. We agree with your opinion. Are there any other theories that the KKS has, that it would like to share with the citizens?'

'Yes, yes, of course! We have several more theories! Captain Kim Young-Chul must have had excellent leadership skills if the chief of TSRS selected him. But what if the chief was wrong? Young-Chul only had a few years of experience, and I see no reason why the chief had to pick him! Young-Chul might not have been able to steer his members away from a crash!'

'Thank you for sharing your opinion. We will look forward to more data from KKS.'

Turn to page number two to read updates about the condition of earth as described by NASA specialists.

The chief threw his tab aside angrily.

"Rubbish," muttered the chief.

He kept rolling and turning around in his chair, unable to keep his irritation down. It was already six in the evening, and the chief usually returned to his house at four. But given the present circumstances, Yohan wanted to stay back. Unfortunately, there was no solution to this — the TSRS had tried to modify their computers, create a different search, and send a couple of rockets to space to find the MN-04 — so far, nothing. He was sipping his coffee now, rolling around in his computer chair, and staring out of the glass window to his back.

The sky was a dark blue today. There were significantly fewer people than usual, walking around, buying essentials. Tiny shops clung to the parapet around the station: some of these were tea and food shops, and some were cloth shops. Older men were the owners of these shops — their faces filled with wrinkles, and their rough, scarred hands were waiting for customers at the shop's counter. The chief's sudden peacefulness at looking outside the window had quickly turned to panic as he heard a call on his tablet.

What would happen now? Would it be a call from Shankar saying that NASA had found something terrible? Was the government telling him to abort the mission and answer the rumours? Was it Ira, continuously asking him questions about the modified computers? The chief thought of the hundreds of things that could happen. He turned to where his table was, looking down towards the tablet — it was a call from an unknown space station.

Yet, in today's age, there was no "unknown space station" in the world. How was this happening? He thought for a few seconds and decided to pick up the call. He could see a blurred image, indicating that it was a video call.

"Hello?" said the chief to the glitched camera, which was an in full screen mode on his tablet.

The camera kept glitching. It was a man's face. Soon, it started becoming even more apparent. The face seemed familiar to the chief.

"Hello?" asked the chief once again. Yohan was starting to think that this was a person calling the wrong number — although he remembered that the tablets could identify a fake number or station. He was getting even more confused. Then, suddenly, the camera was as bright as ever, and the chief was finally able to recognise the face — Idhant!"

That face was tired, and he could see that Idhant was sitting in what looked like an office. The chief had so many questions!

"IDHANT?" yelled the chief. "CAN YOU HEAR ME?"

Idhant didn't answer, but he looked back towards the office door. He kept clicking on several buttons — he couldn't hear the chief.

"IDHANT! IDHANT — CAN YOU HEAR ME?"

The call quickly got cut.

"W-what?" said the chief to himself. But then, he remembered that Ira was still at the station.

"IRA!"

Chapter 25

THE MONG BEACH

The astronauts looked towards Nihaan, who had stood up from his seat with his salad still in his mouth. He looked like a sluggish baby who had just been fed by his mother.

Nihaan had suddenly blurted out his idea without even realising what he had said.

"Y-Yeah," replied Nihaan.

"How can mangoes attract them?" said Femi

"Femi," continued Aveen. "Mangoes are an item they have never seen. We could make them taste one."

Young-Chul narrowed his eyes, thinking.

"Well, we can give it a try," said Young-Chul. "But where do we even get mangoes from?"

"The spacecraft! Yours!" said Nihaan.

"How do we get to our spacecraft, then?" asked Vera.

"Grete might give us permission," said Alf.

Suddenly, the door opened, revealing Grete and his "guards".

"Good afternoon," said Grete, allowing himself to give them a slight smile. "We shall then go to the rivers and coastal areas nearby."

Everyone groaned and made it so Grete couldn't hear it. The aliens took them and walked out of the house. The MN-04 team nodded farewell towards their colleagues. Grete, the aliens, and the astronauts walked out of their prisoner home and took a red-electric bolt.

In a few minutes, they got down — only to see bluish skies above them and water and sand all around them. How soothing it looked! The water, colourless but gorgeous, flowing smoothly along the coastal area. They hadn't seen such smooth currents of water areas along the earth's many coasts in over 20 years. Now, they all stared at the water in awe. The ocean was very attractive — they could appreciate its value as a tourist spot for aliens.

"Beautiful, isn't it?" said Grete. "We aliens always make sure that their surroundings are clean. We do not spoil our precious water, and we do not kill the sea animals that live in the water, even in the shallow areas that we access.

"Do you extract salt from here?" asked Arham.

"No, no, we leave the water just as it is. We do not want to do anything that endangers the quality of our water."

Arham thought that extracting salt wasn't dangerous and wondered why Grete would think such a thing. But he decided not to ask any questions.

"Technically, on earth, we call these areas beaches," said Jacob. "What do you people call them?"

"Interesting question," said Grete. "We call them Naes."

"Naes?" repeated Idhant

"Yes."

"And what is the name of this Nae?" asked Dr Sanghvi. She was surprised that she was saying "Nae" instead of beach.

"The Mong Beach."

Everyone thought it was a strange name, but they didn't want to argue with beings who held all the power.

"Grete…" said Young-Chul. "How did you learn English?"

"Well," said Grete. "When the previous mission members arrived, I actually didn't know any English. Gradually, as they spoke, I managed to pick it up."

"In five years?" said Amelia, who thought five years was significantly little time to learn a language.

Grete nodded.

"Let's go to another place now — the Sang River."

Grete walked towards the electric bolt car, and so did the aliens and the astronauts. It took them five minutes to reach as apparently, it wasn't nearby. Grete took them to see the river and explained its features comparing it to places on earth. They went back to their prisoner home, leading Grete off.

"Hey," whispered Arham to Alf as they got off the electric bolt car.

"Could you go and ask Grete the time?"

"Why not do it yourself?"

"Just do it, please."

Alf mechanically walked towards Grete, who was almost about to enter the electric bolt car.

"SIR!" yelled Alf making Grete yelp.

"O-Oh, were you calling out to me, you — mechanical being?"

"Could you tell me the time, please?"

Grete laughed.

"Yes, of course. In Tian, we consider it thirty minutes past nine now, on Earth — let me see…"

Grete looked towards the vast, thin glass screen in his pocket.

"On Earth, it is twenty-three minutes past five."

"Thank you."

Alf walked towards his team members, and they all went inside. Arham mouthed a thank you to Alf as they walked inside.

"Nice trip?" asked Sidharth soon as the MN-O4 team entered.

Young-Chul smiled.

Chapter 26

ALONE NOW

"We don't need a backup plan to reach the spacecraft. Lately, our plans haven't been working," said Aveen.

"How do we reach the spacecraft, then?" asked Vera.

"Grete might give us permission if we tell him that the mangoes are on the spacecraft," suggested Naaz.

"When should we ask?" said Jacob.

"He will come soon. Maybe tomorrow?" said Alf.

Everyone waved aside the problem temporarily and sat down to have dinner, that had already been placed on the table. They had a light dinner — chicken soup. They ladled it into their mouths out of bowl-shaped spoons that the aliens had given them.

The MN-04 team had crafted a pretty typical routine for themselves, daily:

- Eat breakfast.
- Go out with Grete, have lunch.
- Go out with Grete a second time, return to have dinner, sleep.

It couldn't get any worse.

****

Early the next morning, around seven, the MN-04 team woke up, tired. The astronauts looked around for the other group of astronauts but couldn't find them. Arham was the first to realise that they were missing. He jumped up from his bed and walked towards Young-Chul, who was exhaustedly tossing and turning in his bed.

"Captain?" said Arham, trying to shake Young-Chul awake; the latter wouldn't wake up.

"CAPTAIN!" yelled Arham shaking him even harder. Young-Chul was not in the mood to talk as he kept fidgeting and fighting to open his eyes. Finally, he nodded, allowing Arham to speak.

"The other group of astronauts aren't here."

"What do you mean 'other group of astronauts?'" asked Young-Chul, yawning.

"THE ASTRONAUTS FROM THE PREVIOUS MISSION!" yelled Arham.

Young-Chul bounced up from his bed, looking around. He, too, couldn't see Aveen, Sean, or the others. However, everyone who was part of the Young-Chul's team was there — they were also nervously looking around.

"They are probably in the bathroom," said Young-Chul.

"No, I checked it." replied Arham.

"I see no reason for us to panic right now. Let's search outside."

Everyone stood up at once and left the room. Jacob checked all the bathrooms, Amelia and Alf checked the meeting room and the storage area, and the others looked in all other parts of the house.

They gathered once again.

"No sign," said Femi.

"Can we panic now?" said Arham.

Young-Chul tried to ignore Arham's question.

"Let's check outside."

Young-Chul was heading towards the door when Alf held him by the hand.

"I suggest we all stay inside. Grete might not allow astronauts to come outside without their authorisation."

Young-Chul heaved a sigh.

"What should we do?" said Dr Sanghvi.

"Maybe Grete took them outside to sightsee just like he does us," said Vera.

"But Aveen said that they are not escorted out anymore — not since their first three days on Tian," said Young-Chul.

"We are not sure yet," replied Idhant. "The aliens might come by soon. We can ask Grete once he does."

A few astronauts were against this, as they thought Grete would be enraged by the questions.

"Let's eat our breakfast first," said Young-Chul. Today, their breakfast comprised slices of toast with jam and glasses of an unfamiliar juice, which tasted okay. They all finished their breakfast in a few minutes, sipping on the velvety liquid. Tian's food was excellent.

"So," continued Young-Chul. "Are the mangoes still fresh, Idhant?"

"Yes," replied Idhant. "They're stored in one of the freezer boxes in the storage room."

"And how many are there?"

"Around 40."

"But if this does work — and the aliens like them — 40 wouldn't be enough for them," said Idhant

"We can use our duplicating system," said Femi. The duplicating system was all the rage in the 2040s. Humans popularly used it for duplicating items — therefore, it was a very valuable invention.

"Look there," said Amelia, pointing out a greyish stone sculpture next to another storage room. It was the sculpture of a man with an angry expression on his face.

"I didn't notice that before!" said Alf. "And I always notice everything."

Idhant patted Alf on the back and smiled.

"Is that a statue of Grete?" asked Dr Sanghvi.

Everyone looked more closely at it from their table.

"Looks like it," replied Young-Chul.

The exit door opened. The aliens had come to pick up their breakfast dishes. Surprisingly, Grete was also with them. Usually, Grete would enter the room after the aliens had picked up the trays.

"Looking for your friends?" asked Grete, sneering, as the others stared.

Chapter 27

MANGOES FROM
THE SILENT VALLEY

"Where are the others?" asked Jacob.
"We are much more technologised than you. So, you wouldn't expect us to order you around than to be mindful of what you are doing.

Everyone gulped. Grete couldn't have figured out what they were doing in the office, could he?

"I saw Idhant in our office. Trying to reach TSRS. None of your methods will work with us. We have far- better cameras. We also have hidden cameras and audio surveillance in this room. So, I can hear every word you say here — and all the plans you've been making with the other astronauts. Brace yourselves to stay here for a long time. We will be breaking your spacecraft soon enough."

The astronauts widened their eyes.

"NO," said Young-Chul.

"Give me a good reason why I shouldn't," said Grete, smirking.

"We-we have something precious to give you," said Young-Chul, nervously.

"Is that so? Show it to me."

"It's on the spacecraft. So, you'll have to let us go there to get it."

"On the spacecraft," murmured Grete. "We won't fall for your ruse,"

"It's not a ruse," said Young-Chul. "Where are the others?"

"We believe it would be better to isolate them from you for now. That is, until you give us the object."

"Very well," said Young-Chul, motioning towards his members to go along with the plan. Some of the astronauts shook their heads in repudiation, but they could see Grete's unfriendly face. They knew they couldn't waste time in this room, stuck here forever, just looking at Tian.

Everyone went out of the room, following Grete, towards their spacecraft. They didn't have to take a vehicle; they walked in the ruddy sand. Faraway, they could see the outlying image of their spacecraft, its yellow façade resplendent.

They walked through the sand of the desert for a few minutes, every time coming even closer to the spacecraft. Finally, Grete stopped in front of the spacecraft.

"Go. The aliens will come with you."

The astronauts and the aliens walked up the steep steps and went inside the spacecraft. Everything was still clean and new. The systems, walls, wires, storage boxes, and seats — everything. Idhant ran towards the storage room to find the box with mangoes. Amelia walked inside the storage room, rummaging in all the boxes. Finally, Idhant yelled:

"I found it!"

Amelia went towards Idhant and bent down to the box — it was white and had strips all around. They tore off the strips one by one and opened the box. The mangoes shone in all their glory, looking as fresh as ever, greenish yellow in colour.

Before the mission, many robots had been sent from the TSRS to collect mangoes from the "Great Silent Valley" — an evergreen rainforest situated in the Nigiri Hills in Kerala. It was one of the very few places on earth where many trees and plants still survived. Several decades ago, the world government had planned to build a big dam in the Silent Valley. However, several activists and members of the public had come forward and vehemently opposed the project. They had feared that the dam would flood the Silent Valley, submerging all the trees, plants, and animals.

A long time ago, they had saved the Silent Valley and now the Silent Valley was saving them!

"Do you remember? Raima had suggested that we pluck the mangoes from the Silent Valley!" exclaimed Idhant.

Amelia nodded, remembering when Raima had offered a surprising suggestion to the chief during a meeting. Raima had thought the taste of mangoes could help the astronauts remember the sweetness of earth.

"One is enough for now," said Amelia.

Idhant picked up a single mango from the box and closed it. Then, both the astronauts ran towards the other members.

Everyone gathered around and exited the spacecraft towards Grete. Idhant was about to hand the mango to Grete, when the ground started moving beneath their feet. It kept convulsing violently with each minute. The astronauts tried to hold themselves back, flailing wildly to prevent themselves from falling. Then, a building far away burst into huge flames, and pieces of the building scattered everywhere.

The plumes of smoke rose everywhere, and the fire started to slow down, but not before it seethed in the perimeter of the building.

Grete laughed and exclaimed: "They are dead — once and for all."

Chapter 28

THE SECRET FORMULA

"Dead?" asked Dr Sanghvi.

"Your other astronauts are dead," said Grete, smiling.

"What are you saying? Are you saying that you killed them?" asked Arham, anxiously.

"Yes, yes. We placed a bomb. Waste of time, they were."

Everyone charged towards Grete angrily, but the aliens held them back by their arms, not allowing them to go forward.

"Give me the object now," said Grete.

Idhant lunged forward and threw the mango towards Grete's hand.

Grete laughed once again.

"What is this?"

"Some fruit," said Alf. Tears formed in most of the astronaut's eyes but they fought them back.

Grete took a bite of the mango. His face was difficult to read — they couldn't tell if he liked it or not. Suddenly a message popped up on Young-Chul's device. It was the first message he had received in days! He quickly opened it — to see a message from Aveen. Young-Chul's eyes flew wide open — it could not be!

"We didn't get affected by the fire. We ran away and are currently in one of the buildings — hiding. Give the mango to Grete."

Young-Chul tried to sneak the message towards Idhant. Idhant looked like he was going to burst aloud with happiness, but he controlled himself and whispered the news to the others. The astronauts quickly beamed with happiness. Alf was glowing. Their tears had dried away and they were waiting for their friends to come any time now. No one was dead.

They all looked over at Grete.

The mango was a beautiful one, fresh from Kerala. Even though the mangoes had always been famous in Kerala, the scientists had discovered new modified ones in the 2050s. It had come naturally from the environment and tasted deliciously sweet. It was difficult for anyone to hold themselves back from eating it. These mangoes were exported worldwide and helped people who didn't have water.

"It's delicious," said Grete, smiling. "This is perfect. What is it called?"

"Mango," said Alf.

Grete nodded.

"I want more of this to distribute amongst my people."

"Will you let us go back to earth, then?"

"Of course. We had a deal."

"We only have 40 mangoes," said Femi.

"We can duplicate them," said Grete.

"Then we need to get something in return," said Young-Chul.

"Yes. We will give you water. Isn't that what you wanted?" asked Grete.

Young-Chul nodded.

"But it will only last for 10 years. So, earth should work to get themselves water."

The astronauts nodded in agreement.

"We will not allow any more astronauts to step foot on our planet. Earth should make its own water."

"Yes," said Young-Chul.

Young-Chul suddenly noticed shadowy figures towards Grete's back — he realised that he was looking at a group of people running in the sand, wearing spacesuits. Aveen and the others ran as fast as possible to reach their friends. Grete saw that Young-Chul was happily smiling, looking elsewhere. He turned to look around and was utterly shocked. Grete murmured something in the alien language.

"You cannot let them die again. We gave you mangoes. We are going back with them to earth," said Young-Chul forcefully, walking towards Grete.

Grete had to admit that his "bomb" had not killed the previous mission's members.

"FINE!" yelled Grete. "You give us those mangoes, and I will send the aliens to get water for you!"

Femi went inside the spacecraft and returned with the white box in his hands. He opened the box to show Grete the mangoes inside.

"You need to give us the water now," said Aveen.

Grete slipped something from the pockets of his coat and passed it to Young-Chul. It was a rectangular card, about nine inches all around, and was gold in colour. Something was written on it in thin, white lines.

"A formula card. Use this card. It will activate water for around 10 years."

"Thank you," said Young-Chul.

"We don't thank you for trying to kill us, though," said Sidharth, giving them a disgusting look.

"One more question," asked Young-Chul. "What are we going to say to our chief?"

"Tell him the truth. You can go now. I will kill anyone who sets foot here."

"It was a good experience. Remember my instructions."

They did not give each other a proper farewell — the astronauts and the aliens. On the contrary, there was hatred in their eyes for one another and distrust of what might happen. But the astronauts knew they had made two grand discoveries: they had found aliens — a new living organism — on another planet, something that had been a mystery on earth for decades. And, they had secured water for their dry planet.

Chapter 29

BACK HOME

The astronauts and Alf entered the spacecraft, no aliens at their back anymore. The members of the previous mission looked with awe towards the rocket — after all, five years had passed for them, and they hadn't seen such a modern rocket.

"How are we all going to sit here?" said Aveen, pointing at the seats.

"Half of you can sit in the food area. There are seats there as well," said Young-Chul.

The previous mission's members went to the food area while the others stayed in the system area, maintaining the exact positions as before. Finally, everyone took a seat happily. Surprisingly, no one was hungry — they had eaten enough food on Tian.

Idhant followed the same routine — counting down the time to launch. Then, finally, the spacecraft took off, and the astronauts and Alf filled it with happy chatter all around the spaceship.

"Do you think the chief will believe our story?" asked Dr Sanghvi.

"We will see," said Vera.

Alf unfastened his belt to check on the previous mission's members. He walked into the food area. They, too, were laughing and talking. But Alf noticed an injury on Sean and Dr Abridhanta's leg. The damage didn't seem very serious and looked very recent. Blood was seeping out.

"SIRS!" yelled Alf.

"Is everything okay, Alf?" asked Kiara.

"Why didn't you tell us about the injury!"

Sean and Dr Abridhanta looked at their legs nervously.

"WHAT?" yelled Aveen, standing up

"It's not a big injury," said Dr Abridhanta. "Trust me; we were going to go to the aid room to bandage them up anyway."

"Robot — could you go and get Dr Sanghvi?'

Alf quickly ran towards the other side of the spacecraft, and went towards Dr Sanghvi, who was talking to Amelia.

"Two of the other astronauts have sustained an injury. Please come immediately."

Dr Sanghvi stood up at once and ran towards the other side. Young-Chul and all the others, except for Jacob and Idhant, also ran towards the previous mission's members.

Dr Sanghvi took out a first-aid box from inside her pocket, went towards both the astronauts, and bent down. She fished out an ointment and applied it to the injuries, before rolling up both legs in bandages. She then stood up at once.

"Both of you should have alerted me earlier!" said Dr Sanghvi. "Dr Abridhanta!"

"Yes?" he said nervously.

"I thought you were also supposed to treat the others if they got injured, and yourself too!"

Dr Abridhanta gulped. The sweat poured down his face.

Young-Chul and Aveen couldn't scold them anymore and went towards their seats.

"WAIT!" yelled Young-Chul, alerting the previous mission's members as well.

"What is it?" said Aveen.

"We need to contact the chief!"

Everyone had forgotten about that. So, the astronauts and Alf walked towards the system eagerly and contacted him. The chief answered the phone at once.

"HELLO?' said the chief, almost crying.

"SIR! WE CAN HEAR YOU!" said Aveen.

"OH MY GOD — WHERE WERE YOU ALL? WE HAVE BEEN SEARCHING FOR ALL OF YOU FOR AGES! WHO ARE THE OTHERS AT THE BACK? WHAT ARE YOU DOING? WHAT HAPPENED —"

Raima who was dressed in a regular pair of pants and a denim top propped up in the video call. She was sitting on a desk near the chief and studying, several books scattered on her table. She too, had leaned over and gasped at the astronauts.

"It would be best if you calmed down," said Femi.

"Yes, yes..."

"Sir, we found the previous mission's members on Tian as well!" exclaimed Young-Chul.

"WHAT?"

"Yes," said Young-Chul triumphantly.

"OH MY GOD — AVEEN, NAAZ. HOW DID YOU ALL SURVIVE!"

The chief looked like he was going to cry.

"We will explain everything to you — we will reach earth soon, and we'll talk there, face-to-face. We got water as well!"

The chief seemed too astounded to talk.

"We will talk soon."

"I will send an upgrade to the spacecraft. It will help you to travel faster!" said the chief. "Oh god — I-I hope this isn't a dream!"

Jacob hung up the call.

"What upgrade did the chief give?" asked Naaz.

"He gave us an upgrade of time. We will be reaching earth tomorrow!"

****

It was early the next morning, and the astronauts and Alf had slept soundly all night. They now woke up quickly in excitement. They were going to reach earth in a matter of hours. So, everyone removed their thermal spacesuits and slipped into their everyday suits. They could see earth from their windows — it was still their terrible earth — but they were glad to see it. It was soon going to change into the most wonderful one. They all had breakfast and went back to their seats.

"We are going to reach earth in 30 minutes," said Idhant.

Everyone put on their helmets again and sat back comfortably. Their mood was the best it had ever been in their lives. 20 minutes passed, and they were hurtling down to earth. They could see the blackish clouds forming outside, but the spacecraft was going fast. They all closed their eyes, and when they opened them — they could see the land outside the TSRS. Finally, they reached their station's spacecraft area. Hundreds of people were standing outside; it was evident that the TSRS had told them that the team was coming back with water. All the astronauts, including Alf and the previous mission's members, stepped out of the spacecraft — with people cheering them on. They were the saviours of the planet.

Chapter 30

A BEGINNING

1 January 2060

A lady with strands of white and black hair and round glasses was standing in a house, looking outside the window at the night sky. The city outside was aglow with the bright streetlights. The moon shone even brighter, resembling a tiger's claw. The lady looked towards the stars — taking them in, one by one: they seemed to multiply as she looked across the sky. It was slightly dark at 8 pm, but the streets were filled with people, walking and chattering. Since it was the new year, people had blown up beautiful electric fireworks, in different shapes and sizes. The lady thought that one of the fireworks looked like the structure of TSRS. She gave a smile and walked towards the bright blue sofa next to her. The house where the lady lived was a big mansion that had been left to her by her parents, who had died five years ago.

She sat on the couch with the glass remote in her hand, clicking a button that switch on the TV. The TV was enormous and was made up of glass, making it easier for children to break it. (One must be obliged to tell the reader that scientists at this time are still working on fixing it.) Music arose from the TV — it was time for the News. The News was colourfully designed with pictures, and the editors read the headlines:

2060: A New Year Begins

Marcus, president of the world, gives a speech to the earth's citizens.

Marcus immediately appeared on the screen, standing, and holding a mic in his hand. But unfortunately, the lady had switched on the subtitles and muted the voice — she didn't have time to discern Marcus's fast talk.

"First of all, I would like to say a happy new year to everyone."

The crowd cheered for Marcus.

"Many extraordinary things have happened last year — citizens from all continents have recovered

from the contagious Flamin virus, and more people have helped their societies. I would like to first go back 10 years — to us before earth. That earth was in a dangerous situation — it had no water, many of its citizens were dying. Then, the team on the MN-04 mission and the team before them returned from the alien planet "Tian", bringing us sufficient water for 10 years. Now it's 2060. The alien water isn't enough for us anymore. But our dear astronauts had reminded us that earth's citizens would need to work after this. I could see the people, united in their determination to help the world! We needed to gather; form organisations to build up the earth, which was once beautiful. The astronauts braved great danger to help us realise that this was the only solution — to make all of earth work together. The alien president Grete, had also helped us realise that. We have outstanding, talented citizens on earth to help us whenever in need. We grew flowers on the beautiful crop fields, we pushed down our greatest enemy, global warming, we fought all our troubles! Therefore, now, we are living a great life — we, we have water. I am proud of all the countries who have worked endlessly to get the earth back to what it once was. But we look forward to avoiding any more viruses-like the Flamin. Even though this is the New Year, let us all pray: we should not face another virus like the contagious

CORONA virus, which began in 2019 and ended in 2023.

The crowd laughed at Marcus's humour.

"I will hand over the mic to Chief Yohan now; I wish you a happy new year."

The lady turned off the TV and placed the remote on the wooden table in front of her. She sighed and lay down on the couch. Her stomach grumbled with hunger. She chuckled and decided to grab dinner.

"Ira!" yelled a man — the lady's husband, Advik.

"Yes, yes. I am coming!" exclaimed Ira.

She walked towards the dining area. The dining table was full of people sitting at it — the 2050 MN-04 mission astronauts. All the nine astronauts, including Alf, were there. But, more surprisingly, Raima was there!

"Sorry, I made you all wait," said Ira

"It's okay!" said Vera, smiling. She had grown taller and more enthusiastic about her job.

"Ma'am, were you watching Marcus's speech?" asked Arham, 39 years old now, with a slight beard growing on his face.

Ira nodded.

"He gives the most dramatic speeches!" exclaimed Femi with a smile. Femi somehow looked even taller than usual in his black suit, but his demeanour was the same. Raima laughed. She was a 22-year-old student at the Thumba Space University.

"He always finds something odd to say about Marcus!" said Dr Sanghvi, wearing a white coat — she had just come from the lab.

Everyone nodded.

"You all have terrible manners," said Young-Chul sarcastically. He had grown older, obviously, but nothing could deter him from assuming leadership. His appearance hadn't really changed, however, even though it had been 10 years.

"Bad manners, you said?" asked Jacob. He was still a great pilot.

"Did you make this food, ma'am?" asked Idhant — he was still the early bird but was more talkative now.

Ira nodded.

"Advik and I took turns."

"I guessed that," said Amelia, the American. She now had an Indian accent. Her family was still in America, and she had travelled to Kerala to meet her dear friends again.

"Let's have dinner. The dinner will get cold."

Advik filled everyone's plates with fried rice and chicken — the usual tasty staple for all Indians at a feast. Amelia, Jacob, Vera, Femi and Young-Chul were not new to Indian food — they had already tasted the staples a long time ago and loved it all.

"Alf, why don't you take some more chicken?" said Ira to the robot sitting in the middle.

"Thank you, ma'am!" said Alf, and he grabbed some chicken and put it on his plate.

"He has always held on to his manners, ever since the beginning!" exclaimed Ira.

"Who?" said Arham.

"Alf!" said Advik.

"Yes. He was quite a saviour back on Tian!" said Young-Chul.

"We can all thank Raima for suggesting we pluck those mangoes all those years ago. After all, she has also saved us and earth!"

"Yeah, those weren't some ordinary mangoes. Those were the mangoes from the Silent Valley. The people back then saved the Silent Valley. The valley gave us the mangoes. In exchange for those, the aliens gave us water! If we save Mother Earth, she returns the favour and how!" Exclaimed Raima, smiling.

Ingram Content Group UK Ltd.
Milton Keynes UK
UKHW020802270323
419227UK00016B/949

9 781636 406749